STAR WARS
GUARDIANS
OF THE WHILLS

WRITTEN BY
GREG RUCKA

DISNEY
LUCASFILM PRESS

LOS ANGELES • NEW YORK

For information address Disney • Lucasfilm Press,
1101 Flower Street, Glendale, California 91201.

Printed in the United States of America

First Edition, May 2017

1 3 5 7 9 10 8 6 4 2

FAC-020093-17088

ISBN 978-1-4847-8081-7

Library of Congress Control Number on file

Reinforced binding

Visit the official *Star Wars* website at: www.starwars.com.

SUSTAINABLE FORESTRY INITIATIVE

Certified Sourcing
www.sfiprogram.org
SFI-00993

THIS LABEL APPLIES TO TEXT STOCK

To Eric,
Who is more Baze than he knows.

That which surrounds us, binds us.

In our connection to one, all is connected.

This is the truth of the Force, no more, no less:

Life binds the living.

That which rises must fall, and that which falls must rise.

From the first breath of the infant

To the last breath of the aged,

We are one, together.

—Kiru Hali, Sage of Uhnuhakka
From *Collected Poems, Prayers, and Meditations on the Force*,
Edited by Kozem Pel, Disciple of the Whills

CHAPTER 1

"CHIRRUT ÎMWE," Silvanie Phest said. "We require the assistance of a Guardian."

Chirrut Îmwe dropped his chin against his chest and smiled, but said nothing. Silvanie Phest's voice was a comfort to him, a reminder of better days, and hearing her always gave him pleasure. She was an Anomid, one of a handful she had led from their homeworld of Yablari to Jedha. Anomids had no vocal chords, communicating with one another through a sophisticated and terribly subtle combination of hand and body language that, even were Chirrut not blind, he would never have been able to follow. Outside of the confines of her colony, Silvanie therefore employed a vocoder to communicate, and either through accident or intent the programming on the device had given her voice a delicate and subtle harmonic singsong. Even among the din of NiJedha, Chirrut found her voice soothing. There had been a time when that modulated voice had risen so beautifully in her devotions that every Guardian at the Temple of the Kyber would pause to hear it whenever she sang her prayers.

Then the Empire came to Jedha. The Imperials stripped the Temple of its artifacts, of its history. They barred the doors and posted stormtroopers around the perimeter, forbidding entrance if not forbidding devotion. The Disciples of the Whills who had worshipped so diligently for so long had been cast out, and the Guardians who had watched over them with the same vigilance alongside them. Now, as far as Chirrut knew, all that remained of those who had tended the Temple of the Kyber in NiJedha—in the Holy City—were a paltry handful of Disciples of whom Silvanie Phest was one, and two Guardians of the Whills with nothing left to guard and who were too stubborn to abandon their home.

Or, if you were to listen to Baze Malbus tell it, one blind Guardian and his long-suffering friend.

Silvanie Phest no longer sang, and Chirrut Îmwe missed that.

Chirrut tilted his head slightly, as much to hear

her better as to let Silvanie know he was listening. He turned the smooth alms bowl in his hands, felt the shift of money sliding along its bottom, heard the music of different currencies colliding: Imperial credits and Old Jedha knots and who knew what else. He rarely collected much, but this didn't bother him. Collecting charity was the by-product, not the intent. It was the excuse, and it placed him below the stormtroopers' notice. He sat, most days, to listen, and to learn, and to try—as he had for so long, now—to feel the living Force moving around him.

"At the Temple of the Kyber," Silvanie said. "Along the Old Shadows. There is a man. He will not leave. He is frightening the devoted."

"The Force is all," Chirrut said. "The Force accepts all."

"This man does not come to worship, Guardian Chirrut Îmwe." Silvanie's voice shifted, a melodic half-tone descent that filled her words with unspoken concern, unspoken sorrow. "He brings danger. We fear he will bring violence. We fear he will bring storm-troopers. There are still many who make the pilgrimage, and those of us who are left wish to aid them as best we can. We fear this man will bring death."

"Who is this man?" Chirrut asked.

"He says he is a Jedi," Silvanie said.

Chirrut lifted his chin. Past his left shoulder, he felt Baze Malbus rouse himself from where the big man had been dozing in a precious pocket of warm sunlight.

"No," Baze said.

The word was, in so many ways, the perfect embodiment of who Baze Malbus had become, as blunt and as hard as the man himself. *No* was the word that seemed to define Baze Malbus these days, all the more so since the Imperial occupation had begun. *No*, and in that word Baze Malbus was saying many things; no, he would not accept this, whatever *this* might be, from Imperial rule to the existence of a Jedi in the Holy City to the suffering the Empire had inflicted upon all those around them. *No*, ultimately—and to Chirrut's profound sadness—to a faith in the Force.

"He says the Force is with him," Silvanie said. Chirrut heard her voice shifting slightly, could almost see her turning her head from him to Baze and back as she spoke. "Please, Guardians—"

"Guardian," Baze said. "One. Him."

Chirrut's smile turned to a grin as he felt Baze jerk a thumb in his direction.

Silvanie continued. "We can offer so little to those who come, and this man would threaten even that. And if the stormtroopers hear what he is saying, if they come, it will be the excuse they seek, they will accuse us—"

Chirrut rose all at once, tilting the contents of the alms bowl into one palm, then tucking the bowl itself away within his robes with the other. He reached out, found Silvanie's six-fingered hand with a touch, turned his palm to empty what money he had gathered into hers.

"For food and water," he said. He reached back for his walking stick. "We will come."

"I won't," Baze lied.

Chirrut grinned.

Life in the Holy City had never been easy for any of its inhabitants, but it had not always been cruel. There had always been those who suffered deprivation and hardship, there had always been those who sought to abuse their strength over others and to exploit weakness. There had always been illness, and those who were hungry, and those who went without.

But there, too, had been peace, and generosity, and

comfort, and warmth. There had been families bound by love, and honest beings who did honest work. There had been the respect of sentients for one another, all bound by the understanding that they lived their days in a rare and precious place in the galaxy, a place that meant so much to so many. There had been the devoted attendants of countless faiths, all dedicated to the veneration of the Force in their own ways. From the Brotherhood of the Beatific Countenance to the Phirmists to the Weldsingers of Grace to the followers of the Central Isopter and more, and of which the Disciples of the Whills were but one, though perhaps one of the most prominent due to their place in the Temple of the Kyber.

There had been, as Chirrut perceived it, a balance.

The Empire had ruptured that. It took, and claimed to bring in exchange "order." In truth, Chirrut and Baze both understood this was a lie; the Empire returned nothing. The imbalance rippled in every conceivable way. Where once there had been a steady stream of pilgrims and tourists, now there was barely a trickle. Where once the kyber crystal mines had made modest profit for those who worked them, now the Empire tore open gashes in the surface of Jedha, greedy for more and more. This, in turn, brought more pollution and filth into the atmosphere. Food and clean water, never abundant but always adequate, became scarce, and in some cases toxic. Illness and injuries became commonplace. Medicine and healers diminished.

People grew desperate, and the stormtroopers answered that desperation with violence. Violence was returned in kind. Scattered insurgencies sprang to life, unaffiliated and loosely guided, striking back at the Empire out of anger. The constant sound of the cargo transports overhead was joined by the grind and hum of armored personnel carriers, of the clatter of armor, of the sound of weapons being readied, being aimed, being fired. Homes were destroyed, and the refugees left in their wake did their best to flee, and if they could not flee, simply to survive.

The suffering was everywhere; less for some, greater for others, but touching in some way, in some fashion, all who lived on Jedha.

It made Baze, who had nursed an anger all his own for so long, even angrier.

It just made Chirrut sad, and all the more determined to keep his faith in the Force and to find a way to ease the suffering of those around him.

So he followed Silvanie Phest, and Baze Malbus followed him, as Chirrut had known he would.

The echo-box at his waist clicked away softly, occasionally vibrating, warning him of potential obstructions or hazards in his path. He had worn some manner of the device for so many years now that its constant feedback was almost entirely internalized, to the point that Chirrut was frequently unconscious of what information it was feeding him as opposed to what sensory information he was collecting himself. He could hear Silvanie's long-legged stride, the rustle of her robes, amid the noise around them. He could find her scent, discern it even among the mixed odors floating around them. Another change the Imperials had brought—sanitation suffered as bathing went from a necessity to a luxury. Few people in the Holy City could manage to stay clean, and those who did were almost certainly Imperials. Sweat and dirt and smoke and filth permeated everything, and among them came another odor that Chirrut had not known since he was very young, and had almost forgotten.

The scent of fear.

It was pervasive. It mixed with the odor of frying

food and nearly rotten vegetables sold in market-vendor stalls. It threaded into the smoke of the endless mining, and it rose from the refugees desperate for a way off the moon, and from the stormtroopers encased in their armor who brandished their authority with a coward's bravado. It was everywhere, from everyone.

Despite his best intentions, it even, sometimes, was a scent that Chirrut caught from himself.

But never from Baze.

Silvanie led them along the long-ago-memorized path from the southern-mesa edge of the city, through the Old Market and into the New Market, past the Khubai Shanty and around the Dome of Deliverance, then into the maze of narrow streets called the Blade. Closer and closer with every step to the Temple of the Kyber, where Chirrut had spent so many days and weeks and months and years, and now did no longer. He could hear stormtroopers more frequently as they approached, hear the soft hiss-click of their comms, feel the subsonic rumble of their vehicles on patrol, their numbers growing the closer they came to the ancient center of worship.

Once, Chirrut had heard a pilgrim asking a Disciple just how old the temple truly was.

"How old is the Force?" the Disciple, Kozem Pel, had answered.

Chirrut Îmwe thought that was a very appropriate answer.

It was a cold day, but it was almost always a cold day on Jedha, and Chirrut felt the chill grow as they walked. His sense of place, of direction, of movement, told him that they had turned along the Old Shadows, the long outer wall of the Temple of the Kyber that was forever condemned to remain shielded from sunlight. This, too, had meaning. For the light to exist, there must be the dark. For the Force, there must be balance.

Now he could hear several things at once. A murmur of voices, a mixture of languages, and amid them Basic, the common galactic tongue. He heard Silvanie's pace falter, then come to a stop. He heard the voice of Angber Trel, another of the Disciples who like Silvanie had remained. He heard Baze behind him, a grunt of annoyance.

"That," Baze said in Chirrut's ear, "is no Jedi."

Chirrut stood still, moved his walking stick from his right hand to his left, passed it back, then took hold firmly at the top, feeling the gentle hum of the containment lamp. He wrapped his fingers around the smooth uneti wood of the shaft.

"Please, good sir." This was Trel. "Not here, I implore you. You must stop."

"I will not," a man said. "I cannot! Silence will condemn us!"

"If the stormtroopers hear you, they will—"

"Let them come! I will protect you all! The Force is with me!"

Baze grunted again, unamused.

Staff in his hands, Chirrut lifted his chin, inhaling through his nose, letting his body relax. He felt the street beneath his boots and the staff resting upon it, and he felt the weight of his robes and the touch of the cold air on his skin, on his face, on the backs of his hands. He exhaled, letting himself settle, feeling himself connected to the world around him.

"I am one with the Force," he said, to himself and to the universe at once.

Then he stretched out with his feelings.

Chirrut Îmwe was not a Jedi. He was not, by any definition, a Force user. But what he could do, what he had spent years upon years striving for the enlightenment to do, was—sometimes—feel the Force around him. Truly, genuinely feel it, if only for a moment, if only tenuously, like holding his palm up to catch the desert sand that blew into the city at dawn and at dusk. Be, however fleetingly, one with the Force.

Sometimes it was as effortless as breathing. Sometimes it was as hard as living. And sometimes he could feel the Force, truly *feel* it, moving around him, connecting him to the world and the world to him, the warmth of the light and the chill of the dark, and stretching out further and further, and he could almost *see—*

Then it would slip away, that sand between his fingers again, and he would be left as he had been before. But not entirely. As if a memory lingered. As if the echobox he wore had been somehow tuned, had opened his senses that much further.

This was, in no small part, why Baze's lack of faith caused Chirrut such pain, though Chirrut did his best to conceal this from his friend. Because Baze had lost his faith in something that was beyond Chirrut's ability to even begin to describe, but which Chirrut knew to be manifestly true.

Chirrut stretched out with his feelings, and for a moment it was there again, the elegant interconnectedness, the ineffable bonds among everyone and everything. Their places in space and in time, their lives, their energy. The vibrant cluster of pilgrims and the presence of Silvanie and Angber Trel and the reassurance of Baze, and amid it all, one other, no stronger or weaker than the rest, but occluded, as if moving through shadow or cloud.

He exhaled, lowered his head and his voice with it.

"No," he told Baze. "He is no Jedi."

"That's what I said. I don't need to be one with the Force to know that."

Chirrut heard—or felt, he couldn't quite be certain—the man turn to them, lifting his voice.

"Guardian! Stand with me! We will make the Imperials pay!"

"He means you," Baze said.

"He could mean you," Chirrut said.

"No," Baze said. "He really couldn't."

The man was coming closer. Chirrut tried to locate him more precisely, to focus upon him, and for an instant again it was as if he could feel this stranger, and again there was the sensation that his form was somehow disrupted. Not so much concealed as poorly defined.

"Help me," the man said, and he was close enough

now that he could lower his voice, urgency in his words. "Stand with me, Guardian."

Baze started to move, but Chirrut shook his head slightly, and that was enough, and he felt Baze relax again. Chirrut held out one hand, and the man took it, and Chirrut could feel the warmth of his skin, the texture of tiny scales on his palm, between his fingers. He couldn't determine his species, but that was a matter of idle curiosity only. It didn't matter to the Force, and it therefore didn't matter to Chirrut.

"What is your name, brother?" Chirrut asked.

There was a hesitation. Chirrut felt the man's grip tighten ever so slightly, just for an instant.

"Wernad," the man said.

Chirrut raised his other hand, let his staff rest against his hip, opened his fingers. He felt the man's grip in his hand tremble again, and then felt the warmth of the man's face as he moved into Chirrut's open palm. He felt the man's muzzle, the scales again, smooth and warm; a crease along one jaw, harder, ragged. A scar. He drew a breath through his nose, smelled the man's scent, the city's dust, all the scents of Jedha around him, even the smell of the mines.

"You are angry," Chirrut said. "They hurt you."

The man, Wernad, turned his face against Chirrut's palm, then lifted it free.

"They . . . they have hurt all of us."

"And you would hurt them in return."

"We must fight them."

Chirrut felt Baze shift his stance slightly.

"You claim to be what you are not," Chirrut said. "And you would bring harm by doing so."

Wernad's hand in his tightened again, then pulled free. Chirrut straightened, one hand returning to his staff.

"There can be no peace with them," Wernad said, his voice dropping to a hiss. "There can be no tolerance."

"You put the innocent in danger. Your pain blinds you to this."

Wernad started to turn away, lifting his voice to carry to the others. "They're killing us, they're—"

"How long were you in the mines?" Chirrut asked.

That stopped him. Baze, past Chirrut's shoulder, grunted again.

"They brought you to work in the mines," Chirrut said. "But not alone."

He heard Wernad turn back to face him, the sound of his boots on the ground.

"Was it your family?" Chirrut asked.

There was a long pause. It seemed very quiet, suddenly, though Chirrut understood it was an illusion brought about by the stillness around them. Everyone, the pilgrims, Angber Trel, Silvanie Phest, even Baze, was focused on Chirrut and Wernad.

When Wernad answered, it was almost in a whisper. "My clutchmates," he said. "They are . . . they are one with the Force, now."

"Then they are at peace."

Wernad inhaled, a ragged noise, and Chirrut understood, could almost feel, if not imagine, the intensity of the man's grief.

"I have to . . . the Imperials, they have to . . ."

"Pay," Chirrut said.

"Yes." It was a hiss.

"Not with the innocent," Chirrut said.

"If they follow me, if they believe I am a Jedi, if there are enough of us—"

"Not with the innocent," Chirrut repeated.

"I have to do something!"

Chirrut nodded, then lowered himself to the ground, felt its chill climbing through his robes and into his body. He set his staff across his lap, motioned for Wernad to follow suit. There was another hesitation, then the sound of movement. First Silvanie, then Trel, and then the handful of pilgrims gathered, all of them sitting in the Old Shadows. Chirrut turned his head to where Baze stood, and after another breath—and with a sound that Chirrut could only describe as surly—the big man lowered himself to the ground, as well. Then Wernad was the only one of them still standing.

"Sit," Chirrut said.

"I have to do something," Wernad repeated.

"We are doing something," Chirrut said. "We are keeping faith."

I perceive, in all things, this truth:

That we are forever bound to the Force,

And that the Force forever binds us together.

What we do to one, we therefore do to all.

And thus it is upon us to grant to all

What we would wish for ourselves.

—Karyn I'Yin, Sisters of Sarrav
From *Collected Poems, Prayers, and Meditations on the Force*,
Edited by Kozem Pel, Disciple of the Whills

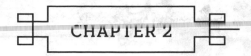

IT WAS AFTER SUNDOWN when they returned to the room they shared off the Old Market, and Baze hit the release on his chest plate and caught the body armor as it fell away from him, tossed it with a flick of his wrist into one corner as he made his way to the sink at the counter. He unhooked the bandolier he used as a belt and sent that after the body armor, shook the shock-stick up his left sleeve free and into his palm, set it down on the surface in easy reach, propped the battered E-5 carbine he carried against the wall. Then he ran the tap, impatiently waiting the requisite thirty seconds before the water turned from rust red to charcoal and then, finally, to something approximating clear. He washed his face, blew dust out of his nose. He wiped his face, then his hands, on his tunic.

Chirrut had taken his accustomed place on the floor near their bedrolls, his legs crossed, hands resting upturned on his knees. His eyes were closed. He had the same small, self-satisfied smile he'd worn since leaving the gathering at the Temple of the Kyber.

"Don't look so pleased with yourself," Baze said.

Chirrut didn't answer.

Baze glared at him, then turned and began yanking open the few cabinets over the counter, searching for something they could have for dinner. On an ordinary day—insofar as there were ordinary days—they would have picked something up just as the Old Market was closing, either a donation from one of the vendors or, just as frequently, purchased leftovers. But while they'd been occupied at the Old Shadows, one of the scattered groups of insurgents had set off an explosive near Gesh's, and while the tapcafe hadn't sustained any damage, the off-duty stormtroopers within had taken it personally. In response, raids had been launched in the Old and New Markets, and the ensuing violence had left stalls wrecked and people scattered. From what Baze had heard on their way back, perhaps as many as a half dozen people had been killed or injured.

It did not help his mood.

"Tea in the middle left drawer," Chirrut said.

Baze shot him another glare, but Chirrut hadn't moved and his expression hadn't changed. Baze hit the release on the indicated drawer harder than he needed to, and the drawer popped open as if afraid of him. This gave him a small moment of satisfaction, which left him just as quickly when he realized the tea in question was Tarine. He put the kettle on, anyway.

"Nothing to eat," Baze said.

"There are those more unfortunate than we."

"That does not make me feel any better."

"Perhaps it should."

Baze started a retort, then stopped. Chirrut was, of course, right, as he so often was about so many things. But that didn't make Baze feel any less angry in the moment, or any less frustrated, and so he set about finding their teacups and slammed each of them down on the counter loud enough to annoy Chirrut but not so hard as to shatter either cup. He stared at the kettle, as if by doing so he could compel the water to reach its boil faster, and when it finally did he filled each cup, put one in Chirrut's waiting hand, then sank down beside

Chirrut and sipped at his own. Some people loved Tarine tea. Baze Malbus was not one of them, and he thought it tasted foul. Its sole benefit, as far as he could determine, was that it was hot and washed the taste of dust and exhaust from his mouth.

"You should sleep," Chirrut said. "We have a couple of hours before we have to go."

"I'm not tired."

Chirrut, who still had not really moved from his meditative pose, brought his cup to his mouth and sipped. His eyes remained closed.

"He was not wrong," Baze said.

"You speak of Wernad, the one in the Old Shadows."

"Yes. He was not wrong."

"Perhaps he was the wrong man to do it."

"Is that your place? To say who will fight and who will not?"

"No more than it is yours to watch over me."

Baze finished his tea, made a face at his empty cup, set it aside.

"They have destroyed our home," Baze said. "They have destroyed the homes of so many others. I understand his rage."

"I know," Chirrut said, and Baze thought that was the end of it, but then Chirrut added, "So do I."

Stormtroopers were garrisoned primarily aboard the Star Destroyer currently in high orbit above Jedha. The massive ship had declared the Empire's arrival, remained above ever since. At night, when the Holy City went dark, Baze could look up and find it in the sky, distant and glowing and constant—an unmoving satellite, like an omniscient, distant eye keeping watch.

The stormtroopers on deployment were shuttled down to the surface either on troop transports or with returning cargo ships after they'd delivered their payloads. The Holy City itself had only a single spaceport, but the facility was overcrowded and out-of-date, built long ago to sustain the pilgrim and tourist traffic to the planet. The very geography of the Holy City made expansion or additional upgrades to the port impossible—the city, built on a mesa rising out of the desert, simply had no room to expand.

The Empire, of course, had assumed control of the spaceport upon arrival. Finding it inadequate to their needs, the Imperials promptly set about clearing an additional four separate locations within the city to use as landing zones and staging areas for their operations. To do this they simply leveled the buildings that stood in their way, with no regard to those residents or businesses they displaced.

Of these landing zones, the largest had been designated LZ-Aurek, and it saw the majority of Imperial military traffic to and from the Star Destroyer parked in orbit. The three other sites were smaller, far more makeshift, and used exclusively to resupply the stormtroopers on the ground, and to load and unload the cargo vessels for their kyber runs.

The Imperial machine never stopped working, and that meant the mines never closed. Even now, well past midnight, Baze watched as the floodlights of one of the smaller landing zones—LZ-Cresh—painted the hull of yet another *Zeta*-class cargo hauler coming in to land. The subsonic rumble of its repulsors kicking over as it came off its main thrusters made dust jump from where it coated the nearby buildings, caught like tiny, briefly lived stars in the reflected glow of the lights.

"That's the one," Chirrut said.

"We'll wait until it's unloaded to be sure." Baze went

to one of the pouches on his makeshift belt, pulled out his set of macrobinoculars.

"That's the one."

"And if it isn't, we'll end up surprising a platoon of stormtroopers."

Baze raised the binocs and adjusted their focus, zeroing in. From their angle—well, more precisely from his angle, as Chirrut had no concern for such things as line of sight—atop one of the nearby buildings, Baze could see past the barricades and into the landing zone. A combat assault tank had pulled in only a couple of moments earlier, stormtroopers taking up position to protect its load of kyber crystals. Baze counted another dozen of the troopers patrolling the perimeter, and an Imperial in an olive-colored uniform whom he took to be the supply master directing operations.

The Zeta completed its landing cycle, sinking down on its landing gear as if the ship were capable of expressing fatigue. Baze moved his gaze to the rear of the hauler, watched the blast of compressed air and steam rise from the rear vents as pressure equalized between the inside and out of the ship. The rear door opened, dropping to the ground with a clang he could hear even from their distance, and which he was certain Chirrut not only heard but felt, as well.

"Well?" Chirrut asked.

"For a man who preaches patience, you could stand to learn some more," Baze said.

"I already told you, that's the ship. *You're* the one who doesn't believe me."

"Chirrut," Baze said.

"Baze?"

"Stop talking now."

"That," Chirrut said, "is the ship."

There was motion, now, around the Zeta. Stormtroopers and uniformed personnel bustling around, using handheld gravhooks to unload crates emblazoned with the Imperial symbol on their sides. Baze saw a uniformed crew member, presumably the pilot, speaking to the deck officer. One of the towering Imperial security droids lumbered out of the back of the ship, and the three appeared to have a brief conversation. More of the uniformed personnel were at the tank, now, unloading the kyber-laden cylinders.

Baze saw no additional security, no additional stormtroopers.

"That's the ship," he told Chirrut.

"I know."

Baze stowed his macrobinoculars and took hold of the E-5. "You are being particularly annoying tonight."

"And there is still so much night left."

Baze grunted. "Can you get down from here alone or should I throw you?"

Chirrut rose, passing his walking stick from one hand to the other.

"I think I can manage," he said.

The reason the Imperials garrisoned their troops aboard the Star Destroyer was for security, nothing more. A garrison on the ground gave any insurgency a possible target; a garrison floating in orbit was untouchable, a sign that opposition to the Empire was futile, and doomed to ultimate failure.

But this created its own set of problems. Troops on deployment needed to be supplied. They needed water, and water was in short supply on Jedha. They needed food, and local food could be poisoned, could be tainted, or could simply be inedible. They needed medical supplies to tend their wounded, be those wounds courtesy of the fledgling and scattered—and, many said, highly ineffective—insurgency or any of a myriad of other hazards. They needed ammunition, because a stormtrooper whose blaster ran dry was as useful as another kilogram of sand in the Jedha desert.

This meant that the Empire needed supply caches throughout the Holy City, secured locations that could serve as depots to reequip and rearm troopers on patrol. Thus, the Empire had exchanged one obvious target—a garrison—for multiple smaller ones, with the logic being that the loss of an occasional cache was insignificant in the face of the continued existence of the larger Imperial presence.

The Zeta that Baze watched land was on a resupply run for these caches, or so Denic, Baze's contact, had assured him. The information hadn't been given out of the goodness of Denic's heart. She'd made it very clear that should any of the resupply cargo, say, fall off the back of a speeder, she expected a cut. Specifically, she wanted any weapons and ammunition that might be recovered.

This was fine by Baze. Weapons and ammunition weren't what he and Chirrut were after.

He waited until Chirrut was off the roof and down on the street before moving himself. Baze was a big man, a strong man, but he knew how to move himself with speed when needed, and with purpose at every moment. While Chirrut's movements had flow, Baze's had direction. He vaulted from rooftop to rooftop, clearing one block and then the next, pausing only for an instant to check on the progress of the resupply. The Imperials had loaded the cargo crates onto the back of an armored landspeeder, a contingent of five stormtroopers responsible for its security. One had the driver's yoke, with another crewing the mounted repeating blaster; the remaining three rode outboard, weapons at the ready, keeping watch.

Baze reached the edge of another rooftop and leapt without breaking stride, this time not to the roof of the adjacent building but instead down to the street. He landed heavy and hard, felt the ground stab back at him, sending pain through his legs to his knees. There had been a time when such a jump wouldn't have given him even the slightest discomfort. There had been a time when he had called himself a Guardian of the Whills, and others had, too. There had been a time when his faith in the Force had been as unshakable and constant as Chirrut's.

He had been a younger man, then.

He drew himself back up to his full height and

checked the E-5 in his hands. He'd modified the weapon himself, trying to draw more power from it, and his efforts had been successful enough that even a glancing shot from the carbine would send a stormtrooper to the ground, and a direct hit could punch a hole through armor and the soldier within it. The trade-off had come in two parts. The first was its ammo capacity. The weapon ate charges, and ate them quickly.

The second was that there was no longer a stun setting.

There was a time when this would have bothered him. He had been a younger man, then, too. These were Imperials, these were the people who had destroyed his city, his home. These were Imperials, who had taken that which was beautiful and made it profane, and it didn't matter if Baze Malbus still *believed* or not; it mattered to him that others did, and he saw the pain the Imperials caused every single day. He saw it in friends and strangers. He saw it in hungry children in the streets, and hiding beneath the smile of Chirrut Îmwe.

It made him angry, but there was still enough Guardian of the Whills in him that he did not want to kill in anger. His balance had been lost long ago, and whether or not the Force was still truly with him, Baze knew that he was no longer with the Force. But he would not kill in anger, not if he could at all help it.

The Imperials made it very hard to commit to that, sometimes.

He drew himself back into the shadows, beneath the covered alleyway between two buildings. He could hear the speeder slowly coming closer, but that was only part of what he was listening for. Then he heard it: the regular beat of Chirrut's walking stick against the road, the *tap-tap-tap* of the uneti wood striking stone.

The speeder lumbered into the street on Baze's right, swaying slightly beneath its load. He pressed himself farther into the shadows, willed himself into stillness as the vehicle passed by. The whine from its engines drowned out the sound of Chirrut's approach, but Baze barely had time to worry before he heard the pitch on the speeder change, the repulsors quieting to an idle. He slid from the alley, looking down the street, and now he was behind the vehicle, and he could see the stormtroopers aboard all facing front, even the one posted at the rear whose job it was to watch their backs.

Chirrut stood in front of the speeder, in the middle of the road. Baze could hear the stormtroopers.

"What's the holdup?"

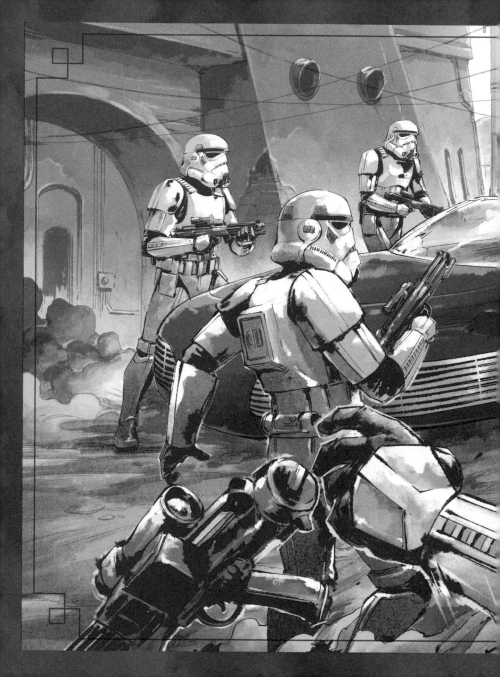

"The guy's blind."

"Move. Move or we'll run you down, citizen."

"My apologies, my apologies," Chirrut said. He bent out of view, apparently searching the ground in front of him. "My stick, I seem to have dropped it. You surprised me, you are on the street so late."

Baze settled the E-5 at his shoulder, exhaled half his air through his nose. The stormtrooper on the mounted gun ran the charger, the clack and whine of the weapon being made ready audible even from where Baze stood.

"Insurgent tricks," the gunner said. He pivoted the weapon down at Chirrut.

Baze fired four times. Four stormtroopers dropped. He sighted on the last, but Chirrut had already moved, had done something with the recovered walking stick, and the last trooper was falling off the side of the speeder.

Baze closed the distance at a run, vaulting into the speeder to find Chirrut sitting at the control yoke.

"Shall I drive?" Chirrut asked.

Denic stood between Baze and Chirrut, watching closely as her crew unloaded the speeder, not speaking. Chirrut stood patiently, hands on his staff. Baze divided his attention between the cargo coming off the speeder and the E-5, which had gone hot where it rested against his leg during the drive to Denic's garage. He'd handed it over to Chirrut, who'd promptly unplugged the charging module without explanation. Now the reason was evident; the whole capacitor system had melted down. Instead of a blaster, Baze now owned a very ineffective club.

He tossed it aside with a grunt.

Denic jerked her head around to him, almost snarling. "Quiet."

Baze shrugged. That the Imperials were out in search of the stolen cargo was a given, but he and Chirrut had been as quick and efficient and quiet—relatively, given the four shots—as was possible, and there'd been no race to hiding, no fear of being pursued as they made their way to the garage. Tomorrow would be different. In the daylight, the Imperials would descend with their iron fist. Tomorrow would be a hard day for much of the Holy City.

He hoped it would be worth it.

It took less than four minutes to determine that it was.

You say:

I cannot name the nameless,

Nor praise the unknown,

Nor swear upon that I do not understand,

When all ends in Death.

And I say:

Then you are not alive.

—Aurek, Pupil of the Central Isopter
From *Collected Poems, Prayers, and Meditations on the Force*,
Edited by Kozem Pel, Disciple of the Whills

CHAPTER 3

"IT'S TARINE," Killi Gimm said. "I'm afraid it's all we have."

"Tarine tea would be very nice, thank you," Chirrut said.

There was a pause that almost became awkward before Baze said, "Yes. That would be nice."

Chirrut grinned.

"Please sit," Killi said. Her voice was soft, raw, and hoarse. "It won't be a moment."

Chirrut found his way to a stool, rested his staff against the high table near his thigh, sat. He set his hands on the tabletop and spread his fingers, letting his palms press lightly against the cool metal. He could feel the subtle vibration of movement around him through its surface, the stronger shivers as Baze moved past him, settling his bulk on a neighboring seat. Other hints of motion, of sound, of life, spread out from where Chirrut sat—Killi, moving through the large, empty kitchen, and out beyond into the common room, where her sister was attending to the orphanage's children, and even the children themselves, the sound of their voices, their play. One of them laughed.

His smile grew. It had been a while since he had heard a child's laughter.

Killi coughed. It came up suddenly, hard and dry and from high in her chest, and the first opened a floodgate for more, and he heard the sound of crockery clattering on a counter, and he started to rise, but Baze was already up and moving to her. Chirrut sat back down. His smile had vanished.

"You are still having trouble breathing," he heard Baze say.

Killi drew a breath, held it a fraction longer than needed, and Chirrut knew she was fighting back another bout of coughs. When she exhaled, he could hear her wheezing.

"I do not like wearing the mask indoors," Killi said. "It reminds the children of the stormtroopers and frightens them. I think we can all agree that they have been frightened more than enough."

"It has gotten worse," Chirrut said.

"The fear? Or my breathing?"

"Chirrut means both," Baze said. "Sit. I'll do the tea."

"It's bad some days." Killi Gimm sat on the stool Baze had vacated. "Better others."

"What day is today?" Chirrut asked.

"Do not make me laugh, Chirrut Îmwe," she said. "You'll make me cough again."

Chirrut reached out to find her hand, and she laced her fingers through his. "The Force is with me, and I am with the Force," he told her.

"And I fear nothing, for all is as the Force wills it," she concluded. He felt her hand on his sleeve, an affectionate squeeze of his arm, before she slipped her hand free. "Though of late, the will of the Force has been harder to discern."

"Understanding the will of the Force was always far more your place than ours, I think." Chirrut turned on the stool, orienting more fully to her. "Disciples always seemed the better listeners."

"And Guardians the better observers, and thus we had a proper balance."

He could hear her smile in the words, and for a moment, Chirrut thought he could discern the Force moving around them, around her. Yet somehow it seemed more tenuous surrounding Killi Gimm. He knew Baze was looking from her to him and back, could feel the weight of his concern, the gentle pressure of his sorrow.

"So concerned you both are!" Killi said. "It is all the dust, nothing more."

"Drink," Baze said, and Chirrut smelled the tea, the touch of the steam as one cup was placed in front of him, the other in her hands. "Slowly."

Chirrut waited until he had heard Killi take a drink, then said, "There was medicine with the food and the water we took from the Imperials. Baze said several doses of the Respitic. It could help."

"It *will* help," Killi said. "Kaya is already giving it to the children."

"Save some for yourself," Baze said.

"The children are more important."

"There is enough," Baze said.

"No," Killi said. "There is enough at *this* moment, Baze Malbus. But in a week? And each week there are more children, and they cough through the night, some of them. Every week there is less food to feed them, less water to drink. So at this moment, I will go without, because soon enough another's need will be greater."

"She sounds like you," Baze told Chirrut.

"No, he sounds like me," Killi Gimm said. "Where do you think Chirrut learned it?"

Before the Empire had arrived, there had been no real orphanage in the Holy City. Before the Empire had arrived, there had not been a true need for one. Children left orphaned through accident and tragedy had almost universally been cared for by other families in the community or, in some cases, by members of one sect or another, brought to live in the Dome of Deliverance or at the Temple of the Kyber or the Waiting of Night or any of the other places of worship. Between the community of faith and the community of the Holy City itself, there had always been someone willing and able to help.

Now the temples were barred and the communities of faith scattered, and where there had been homes and families there were refugees and orphans. Every day there were more of each. Refugees displaced by the Imperial occupation. Children orphaned by the slave labor of the kyber mines, their parents crushed or buried or worked to death under the Imperial boot. Children orphaned by stormtrooper blasters or insurgent bombs. Children orphaned by parents who had managed to steal aboard a freighter or a transport, desperate to flee Jedha, leaving with every intention of returning for their families once they had made it to safety, to security, to freedom.

Chirrut had yet to hear of any who had actually come back.

Killi Gimm had been one of the eldest of the Disciples of the Whills when the Empire came. Her sister, Kaya, ten years younger, had run a small droid repair bay out of her home near the Midwalls, mostly catering her services to pilgrims and tourists alike. Chirrut suspected it had been Killi who had come up with the idea of turning her sister's home into an orphanage. He also suspected Kaya had needed very little convincing. He was certain that neither had understood the magnitude of what they were undertaking when they began.

There were almost a dozen children in their care, now, the youngest just six, the eldest not yet eleven. Many had sustained injuries or suffered illness. All of them needed to be fed, clothed, kept safe, kept warm.

All of them needed attention, needed love. Most of them were human, but by no means all, and this in turn meant that Killi and Kaya had to become familiar with the dietary needs of Rodians, or the sleeping habits of Twi'leks, or the atmospheric requirements of Morseerians.

The things that they could provide, Killi and Kaya provided in abundance. Their attention, their affection, their care. It was in the more material things that they suffered, as all of Jedha was suffering—there was not enough water, and never enough food. They were short of blankets, of credits, of power, of medicine.

It had been Baze who'd said aloud what Chirrut had begun to consider.

"The Imperials," he'd said one evening as he and Chirrut sat over an evening meal of exceptionally bland vesti noodles, "have everything the orphanage needs and more."

Chirrut had just smiled.

Last night had been the fourth such resupply they had intercepted over the last several months, and the necessity of such behavior weighed on Chirrut. Not with regret or guilt, but rather the same sadness he found himself so often confronting. What they had done, they had done for the best of reasons. What they had done, they had done with efficiency, and in that, mercy. That stormtrooper was not the first sentient Chirrut had separated from his life, and he knew without question he would not be the last. He was at peace with the necessity of their actions, but that did not mean he took pleasure from them.

It was of no small comfort to him that Baze, for all their disagreements, felt the same way.

The common room of the orphanage served triple duty as play area, infirmary, and classroom, and it was in the last of these that they found it currently employed. Killi led them to wait just outside the door as Kaya finished the day's lesson. Killi's sister taught with the assistance of an old CZ-model tutor droid, and Chirrut could hear its servos whining as it moved about the room. He could hear the children, too, and it troubled him. There was no fidgeting, no murmuring, no whispering. They answered with soft voices when called upon, and some would not answer until encouraged several times. A couple, not even then.

Chirrut could also hear the sounds of labored

breathing, the high-pitched whisper-whistle of air being drawn into and released from tormented lungs.

They waited until Kaya had finished and the CZ droid took over, leading the children out into the canopy-covered courtyard at the heart of the building for a recess. It was, Chirrut knew, too small a space for so many children, but allowing them out into the street would be too dangerous. He tilted his head, lifted his chin slightly, straining to hear anything that sounded like laughter or joy from outside. He had to wait for it, but when it finally came it gave him such a simple and pure pleasure that he wanted to laugh, as well.

Amid everything, children could still play. Surrounded by suffering, in the shadow—literally—of the Empire, breathing air that hurt their lungs, yet they could still play.

"You didn't have any trouble?" Kaya asked once she was assured the four of them were alone. "With the Imperials?"

Baze grunted.

"I'm sure Killi already thanked you," Kaya said. "But I'm going to thank you both, too."

"How long will the supplies last?" Chirrut asked.

"If we're careful, two, perhaps two and a half weeks."

"We will get more before then," Baze said.

"I'm worried about how the Imperials will respond if you do."

"They will respond the way they always respond. They'll look for someone to punish."

"Doesn't that worry you?"

Chirrut shook his head. "They see it as theft, not charity, Kaya. So they look to thieves as the guilty."

"And with the Empire's arrival, there are plenty of thieves about," Baze added. "They create the problem, they can solve it."

"Eventually they will realize what's really going on."

Chirrut thought Kaya sounded resigned, then reconsidered. What he took for resignation, he realized, was actually regret.

"Do you wish us to stop?" he asked.

There was a silence, broken only by the sound of the children outside. Chirrut understood that Kaya and Killi were passing some manner of unspoken communication—looks, perhaps.

"It is not that we wish you to stop," Killi said. "It is that we are concerned where this will end."

"We will continue for as long as we can," Baze said.

"And after that?" This was Kaya. "Should the worst happen? Should you or Chirrut be captured or killed?"

"What would you rather we do?" Baze asked.

Another pause. Then Killi's voice. "That is the problem. For as long as the Empire remains here, we are trapped in this cycle."

"Then we must find a way to break the cycle," Chirrut said.

"Yes," Killi said. "Before the cycle breaks us."

In darkness I fol-

-low the light and find my way

to the beginning

again,

and again,

and again

—Sajar Ohmo, Clan of the Toribota
From Collected Poems, Prayers, and Meditations on the Force,
Edited by Kozem Pel, Disciple of the Whills

CHAPTER 4

"I NEED A NEW BLASTER," Baze said.

"Use your old one," Chirrut said.

"No."

"You still have your old one."

"Yes."

"So use your old one."

"No."

Baze and Chirrut split without breaking stride as a clump of urchins, each of them so filthy and caked with dirt they left puffs of dust in their wake, barreled past them. Baze kept a hand on the pouch tucked beneath his tunic where he kept his credits, and an eye on Chirrut at the same time, knowing full well it was unnecessary and yet doing it all the same. The fact was, of the two of them, Baze was the more likely to have his purse lifted and not even notice.

"The old one works perfectly well," Chirrut said when they'd fallen back in, side by side.

"The old one is a Guardian's weapon. And I am no longer a Guardian."

"Then you are making a choice."

"Yes," Baze said. "My choice is to find a new blaster."

"No, your choice is to be stubborn."

"My choice is to use a reliable blaster rather than an archaic lightbow."

"Your reliable blaster has proven to be unreliable."

"Which is why I need a new gun."

"Use your old one."

Baze came to a halt in the middle of the street and Chirrut, too, stopped almost instantly, as if he'd been expecting this.

"Like so many conversations with you," Baze said, "we are now back where we started."

"You noticed that, did you?"

"You're very lucky I'm your friend, you know that?"

"I do know that," Chirrut said. "Though I wonder why you are saying this right now."

"I'm saying it right now because I'm wondering why anyone would bother to put up with you."

"Ah," said Chirrut. "I often wonder the same thing about you."

Baze roared with laughter, loud enough that the crowded street took notice of them, including two helmeted and robed worshippers of the Central Isopter, who stepped curiously closer. Baze grinned big at them, showing his teeth, and they stopped, then stepped back, then turned away to melt back into the crowd. Baze took the opportunity to check around them before starting forward again. Chirrut immediately kept pace, his staff extended at an angle to the ground in front of them, swaying slightly from side to side.

"Do you want to go shopping?" Chirrut asked. "Is that what you're saying? Though I doubt we can afford anything that will suit your purposes."

"No." The thought was vaguely absurd to Baze. "That's not how you find the right weapon, you know better than that."

"As we have established, apparently I do not."

"We're being followed."

This seemed to amuse Chirrut. "Really?"

"Since we left the orphanage. I wasn't sure until just now. Two of them."

"Imperials?"

"I don't think so. One is a Twi'lek."

"One?"

"There are two, I think. The other is a Sabat."

"That does not sound Imperial."

"I want to know why they're following us."

"You should ask them."

"I'm going to."

"Now?"

"Soon," Baze said.

They rounded a corner out of the Old Market and continued another couple of blocks, heading roughly in the direction of the Eastern Wall, neither of them speaking. They continued to be followed, and Baze concluded a couple of things from this, not the least of which was that the Twi'lek and the Sabat knew what they were doing. They gave each other space, as well as leaving room between themselves and Baze and Chirrut. This meant that they had to be in communication with one another, either via comlink or hand signals or similar. That meant some degree of training, some degree of experience. If they were criminals, they were of a better class than Jedha normally had to offer.

Why criminals would be targeting him and Chirrut was its own question. The best a robber would get was disappointment. The worst was broken bones, if not from Baze's fists, then from the frightening accuracy and speed with which Chirrut could use his staff.

So not criminals, and well trained, and careful, and that meant they had to be members of one of the insurgent groups working in the city. But this was puzzling on its own, as most of the Holy City's insurgent groups were composed of locals, and locals were predominantly human. Twi'leks weren't a terribly uncommon sight, to be sure, but the Sabat was another matter. The last time Baze had seen a Sabat he had still called himself a Guardian of the Whills, and that had been a long time ago.

They entered a mixed residential and business neighborhood known to the locals as Hopper Town, the reason for the name long since lost to the ages. The squat buildings here stood shoulder to shoulder, with alleys between them so narrow Baze could only make his way through them moving sideways. They turned north, and Chirrut stopped abruptly, holding out a hand to block Baze's progress. Before Baze could ask why, he saw what his friend had somehow already sensed.

Ahead of them, rounding onto the far end of the street, came a patrol of stormtroopers. A half dozen of them leading on foot, their blaster rifles carried at the ready, and behind them a GAV in support, one of the armored personnel carriers, a heavy repeating blaster mounted atop and the gunner visible in his position. Baze glanced around to the narrow alleyways on either side and then up to the balconies and rooftops of the buildings surrounding them. Shutters were slamming into place, and people were hurrying to clear the street.

"There is going to be violence."

Chirrut said it with a certainty that Baze had long ago come to trust absolutely.

"Stormtroopers," Baze said. "Hunting party. This way."

He moved left, to the widest of the alleyways in sight, Chirrut with him. From up the street, he heard the crackle of stormtrooper voices but was unable to make out their words.

"What was that?"

"They are telling everyone to stay where they are," Chirrut said. "We do not want to do that."

"No, we don't. Here, you go first."

Chirrut extended his hands, walking stick in one of them, and felt the walls that formed the mouth of the alley.

"You will not fit," Chirrut said.

"Of course I will fit."

"I am not leaving you behind."

"You are not leaving me behind, you're getting into the alley, Chirrut."

"You first."

One of the stormtroopers had seen them, was pointing in their direction. There were still a good twenty, twenty-five meters between the approaching patrol and where Baze and Chirrut now stood at the mouth of the alley. Baze considered the situation. It was entirely possible that the Imperial patrol had nothing to do with them, was a show of force in response to any number of other things that might have happened, or were happening, in the Holy City. It was also entirely possible that something had gone wrong the previous night, and that a security camera or a witness had seen them hijacking the resupply shipment, and had passed their descriptions along to the garrison. It was also possible—and Baze thought this the most likely—that this was nothing but bad luck, and that the simple act of attempting to leave the street had labeled them as suspect.

The problem was that if they were stopped for questioning, or brought in, there was no telling where that might lead or what it might lead back to. Unlike Baze, Chirrut still dressed as a Guardian of the Whills. He would be singled out because of this, subjected to more questions. And Chirrut, being Chirrut, would not tell the stormtroopers things they wanted to hear, and Chirrut, being Chirrut, would very likely begin spouting the litany. They would detain him. They might even detain him aboard the Star Destroyer, and Baze knew very well that those detained aboard the Star Destroyer were never heard from again.

Baze sighed.

"Fine," he said, "Me first."

He shoved Chirrut into the alley.

"I'll catch up," he said, then started running back in the direction of the Old Market with the shouts of stormtroopers—and his friend—chasing after him.

Whomever, or whatever, the stormtroopers were hunting for, they were out in force, and it seemed to Baze there wasn't a street or square he could turn onto without glimpsing white armor smeared in dirt and dust, or catching an echo of amplified voices from within helmets, or feeling the thud and clatter of an AT-DP walker stomping along a nearby block. Twice, he nearly ran into patrols as they were clearing houses and businesses, and each time he turned away at the last moment, managed to duck into cover before being spotted.

Ultimately, he ended up at Denic's garage. She was not entirely pleased to see him.

"Go away, Baze," she told him.

"I will," Baze said. "In a little while."

"You bring heat with you, man, nova-hot. I don't want to get burned."

That didn't deserve an answer, and Baze's look told her as much. She met his stare, tried to match it, then finally gave up with a snort. She shoved the pair of Torjeka scanner goggles she always seemed to be wearing up onto her forehead, eyed him with raw suspicion. They were a holdover from her piloting days, which some people claimed had actually been her smuggling days. Still others said that those smuggling days had been pretty good days indeed until she'd burned one too many bridges in the Corporate Sector.

Baze didn't know how much of what was said about Denic was true, but he was certain that she had been, once upon a time, a pilot herself. She'd arrived in the Holy City shortly before the Imperials had, and Baze had made her acquaintance entirely by accident in the New Market one day as she'd been arguing with a vendor about the quality of the meiloorun fruit he was selling. They had purple rinds, rather than the more traditional orange-yellow ones, and Denic was insistent they weren't meilooruns at all. Baze had listened for a few minutes before explaining that, in fact, the purple rind was a variant, a hybrid favored by the Brotherhood of the Beatific Countenance. Denic had found this hard to believe.

He'd seen her again the week after the Empire arrived, from a distance, perched on the rooftop of one of the New Market buildings, watching the initial Imperial deployment. There'd been a tremendous amount of air traffic that day, TIEs and *Sentinel*-class shuttles in a constant stream from the Star Destroyer to the surface. She'd watched with her goggles over her eyes, motionless for the better part of an hour, until Baze had left Chirrut alone long enough to go and see what was up with all that. He'd climbed onto the rooftop and sat beside her, and she hadn't acknowledged his arrival for several minutes.

Then she'd suddenly said, "Academy pilots, all of them, you can tell. No flair to their turns. Watch."

Baze had watched, and been utterly unable to see whatever it was Denic was seeing.

"Scrubs, all of them. I mean, they know their jobs, but they've got no passion beneath their wings," she'd said.

She'd gone silent again, and stayed that way, and when Baze had made his way down and back to Chirrut and looked, she had still been on the rooftop, still watching. It was the kind of dedication he had seen in the Temple of the Kyber from some of the Disciples, the absolute focus, absolute commitment of a true believer. He had decided then and there that Denic's faith was flight.

"You two really poked the rancor this time," Denic was saying.

That brought Baze back to the moment. "This is for our benefit?" he asked.

"That is my impression."

"All this over food, meds, and water?"

"You didn't even look in the other crates, did you?"

"They were yours, that was the deal." Baze shrugged. "We got what was needed."

"You two hit a full resupply for LZ-Cresh, Baze. Yeah, you scored rations and meds, but you also boosted their munitions. Some serious stuff."

"You still have it?"

"That's my point. I still have *all* of it. It's too hot to move. I can't even get Gesh or the Tulava Quartet to touch any of it, not yet."

"Where?" Baze asked.

Denic chewed the corner of her upper lip, eyes narrowing. She blackened the skin around each eye out of habit, as if overzealously applying makeup, but for reasons that had nothing to do with the cosmetic. The Torjeka goggles she liked to wear offered numerous benefits, both macro and micro visual settings, as well as thermal, light-enhancing, and electromagnetic views. But they were old, and their seals had weakened, and so she darkened her skin in an attempt to make their lenses appear brighter.

She jerked a thumb over to the far corner of the garage, where a heavy tarp was draped over a vaguely lumpy and speederlike shape. When Baze lifted the corner of the tarp, he saw there was, in fact, not one speeder but rather the bits and pieces of several, and beneath them five of the crates they had taken off the stormtroopers the night before. The crates had been hastily repainted in an attempt to hide their Imperial markings. Baze climbed up over the pieces of dismantled speeders and reached down and wrenched the top off each crate, one at a time. He looked at the contents of each for several seconds without comment, then over to Denic.

"Yeah," Denic said. "You could do a lot of damage with that stuff."

"I like that idea," Baze said.

"Whoa whoa whoa, wait a fraction, big guy." Denic trotted over, but Baze was already hoisting one of the crates up and out of where it had been nestled, and she had to stop and then step back as he set it on the ground between them. Her eyes widened for a moment at the display of strength. "That's my cut, that's the deal. You get the meds, the rations, I get everything else. Remember?"

Baze reached down into the crate, freed its contents from the restraints holding it securely in place, straightened. Denic took another step back.

"That's, ah . . . that's a support weapon, big guy.

They mount that kind of thing on vehicles, it's not . . . that's not a personal weapon, you know? Like, not for personal use."

Baze turned the gun in his hands, checked its heft. It was heavy, though not so heavy that it was uncontrollable in his hands. He looked back into the crate, where the coolant tank and charging belt for the weapon were still resting. He looked at Denic. He grinned.

"I like it," he said.

"Baze."

"Can you rig me something for the coolant tank?"

"Baze, that is a Morellian 35c repeater. It's not even a blaster, you get me? It's technically a *cannon*."

"I can wear the tank on my back. But to do that I will need a harness. Something secure."

"It's like I'm talking to a wall." Denic shook her head slightly at him, then sighed and pulled her goggles back down over her eyes. She peered into the crate, then took another step back. "Well, get it all unpacked, at least."

Baze set down the gun and removed the rest of the contents from their packing. Denic went to the nearest workbench, grabbed her pouch of tools and adhered it to her hip, then returned and squatted on her haunches, examining the tank and charging belt. Baze went back to examining the gun.

"Fully automatic?" he asked.

"Two modes," Denic said. "Full auto, yeah, and then there's a single-shot power mode, pump action, high yield. There should be an electroscope in the crate, too, smart targeting system. Though unless you're chipped or wearing power armor, you're going to have a harder time getting that to work. Fully charged, that thing can spit close to forty thousand rounds before needing a reload."

"Forty thousand rounds, fully automatic." Baze lowered the rifle. "Why do they need that much firepower?"

Denic looked up at him, eyes now hidden behind her goggles.

"Crowd control," she said.

It was well after nightfall when Baze made it back home, now wearing the rig he and Denic had worked up, the rifle in his hands. The rig was a combination of body armor and harness, the coolant tank riding at his back, low enough not to throw off his center of balance. There were only two downsides to the weapon system that Baze could see. The first was that it was nearly impossible to conceal. The second was that the charging belt that ran from the blaster cannon to the coolant tank ran the risk of snagging on potential obstructions. Neither of these was a problem that Baze felt outweighed the benefits of having a weapon that would do what he needed it to do.

That it was a weapon the Imperials might have intended to use on the civilian populace of Jedha only made the potential of using it on them instead all the more satisfying.

He came through the door, saying, "Chirrut, I found a new gun."

Then he saw the Twi'lek and the Sabat who had been following them earlier, both with a cup of Tarine tea in their hands, sitting on the floor on either side of Chirrut. Since he couldn't point the weapon at both of them at the same time, he settled it on the Sabat. The Sabat didn't move except to narrow his already small eyes to vicious slits.

"Resist, please, the urge to use it," Chirrut said.

There was a decidedly awkward pause.

"You made them tea," Baze said, finally.

"It seemed polite."

"Did they tell you why they were following us?"

The Twi'lek cleared his throat. He was extraordinarily tall, evident even with him sitting down, but more than that, he looked decidedly unhealthy. His lekku were emaciated, thin to the point that they appeared brittle, as if Baze could have snapped them from his head with barely any effort. His skin was pulled taut against his skull, and on a healthy Twi'lek the hue would have been almost ivory, but on him it held a pallor more appropriate to a cadaver. His lips were full and glistened a dark reddish brown like dried blood, and in combination with the rest of his appearance this only served to make him appear even more ghastly. He sat with a long electrostaff across his lap, but he made no attempt to grab it.

"You are Baze Malbus," the Twi'lek said. "I am Beezer Fortuna. This is my colleague, Leevan Tenza. We come with an invitation."

"We're on the same side," the Sabat, Tenza, said. His voice had a distinct rasp, as if each word had been dug out of Jedha's own kyber mines, and then had to pull itself, centimeter by centimeter, to the surface, cracked and dirty fingernails and all. Opposite the Twi'lek, he seemed positively short, though similarly hardened and unhealthy. His tunic was stained, showing evidence of frequent and hasty repairs. He wore bandoliers of ammunition crisscrossed across his chest and a further belt of rounds about his waist, but Baze could see no obvious sign of a weapon. A thin sliver of wood jutted from the corner of the Sabat's mouth, and when he drank his tea, the toothpick stayed put.

"What side would that be?" Baze asked.

"The side that hates the Empire," Beezer Fortuna said. "As we have been explaining to your friend."

Baze held his aim a fraction longer, then hefted the blaster cannon so its barrel pointed more to the ceiling than at the Sabat. That there were sentients in the galaxy fighting the Empire wasn't news; there were scattered pockets of resistance that seemed primarily confined to the Outer Rim worlds. Mostly it was word of mouth, rumors, but once in a while something more substantial broke through the Imperial noise. Images from Cherridan, where an uprising at an Imperial labor camp had been brutally put down; reports of a successful assault on the stormtrooper garrison at Winter's Edge; a garbled transmission out of Lothal filled with defiance and hope and inspiration.

The Empire, of course, downplayed such things or dismissed them altogether. Propaganda by enemies of the Empire, it claimed. Lies spread by traitors and saboteurs who threatened the order and peace and security the Empire provided.

One only had to look outside, at what had happened to the Holy City, to know the truth.

"Rebels," Baze said.

Tenza sneered. "True rebels. The ones who will do what must be done."

Baze looked to Chirrut. Chirrut seemed to be studying his tea, which, of course, he could not possibly be doing. He seemed calm as ever, unperturbed by any tension that Baze's arrival might have caused.

"If thinking of us as rebels is a problem," Fortuna said, "you might rather call us 'emissaries.'"

"Emissaries for who?" Baze asked.

Fortuna and Tenza exchanged a look. The Sabat produced a comlink from a pocket, keyed it twice, but said nothing. Fortuna used his staff to get to his feet. Standing, he was a full head taller than Baze, and had to duck his head to keep from hitting it on the low ceiling.

"We will take you to him," Fortuna said. "He is eager to meet you both."

There is no Emotion, there is Peace.

There is no Ignorance, there is Knowledge.

There is no Passion, there is Serenity.

There is no Chaos, there is Harmony.

There is no Death.

There is the Force.

—Anonymous, "The Jedi Code," also known as
"The Jedi's Meditation" (apocryphal)
From *Collected Poems, Prayers, and Meditations on the Force*,
Edited by Kozem Pel, Disciple of the Whills

CHAPTER 5

A SPEEDER PULLED UP for them the moment they stepped out into the night, and Fortuna and Tenza waited until Chirrut and Baze had climbed aboard before joining them. Chirrut couldn't get a sense of the driver beyond the fact that there was one. Male, female, species, all these things evaded him, as whoever was driving didn't speak. He sat with his staff resting on the floor of the speeder, between his knees. Baze was on his right, the heavy presence of the one who called himself Tenza behind him, and the somewhat lighter presence of Fortuna ahead of him, by the driver.

He wasn't certain what to make of things, and as he often did in similar situations, Chirrut opted for patience. What little he could perceive through the Force confused him. None of those around him seemed to bear any immediate ill will, but all carried with them the coils of the dark side. This was not a moral evaluation, but a fact. The Force moved among all living things, light and dark alike. In the orphanage, light had clung to Kaya as she nurtured the children; dark had risen about Killi as she labored through her coughing fits. All Chirrut could be certain of was that Tenza and Fortuna and the driver were warriors of a sort; that they had taken lives, or were willing to do so, or both; and that in this they were no different from Baze and him.

The speeder's engines shifted tone, repulsors switching from hover into motion, and he felt the vehicle jolt forward, bank sharply, then accelerate quickly. The night was already cold, and the wind blowing on him made him all the colder, and he felt the air and the dust in it on his face, snapping his robes.

"We're going outside," Baze told him.

Chirrut understood. They were leaving the city, going into the desert, and a moment later he felt his stomach lift as the speeder dropped, and he knew they were off the mesa and headed to the desert floor. The engines grew louder, angrier, and he felt their speed increase, and beside him, he felt Baze twisting around in his seat.

"Nice night," Chirrut said.

Baze laughed. Nobody else said anything.

"So you got yourself a new weapon," Chirrut said, mostly to make conversation. "Are you happy now?"

"No," Baze said. "I will be happy when I get to use it."

It was Chirrut's turn to laugh.

They rode out into the desert for almost an hour, far enough from the city that Chirrut wondered if what he suspected was caution was, instead, paranoia.

At length the engines lowered their pitch, and the speeder slowed, then came to a stop.

"Where are we?" he asked Baze.

"We are in the middle of nowhere. They clearly do not trust us enough to take us to their base of operations."

Fortuna spoke. "Trust is earned."

"You approached us," Chirrut said.

"Which is why we are here. You may get out."

Baze led the way, reached back to guide Chirrut

out of the vehicle. As soon as Chirrut had his feet on the ground once more, Baze's hand was gone. Chirrut planted his feet firmly on dirt, squared his shoulders, lifted his head. He breathed, the walking stick in his hands pressing hard into the ground.

"Head that way," he heard Tenza say. "You don't want to keep him waiting."

"He will wait," Baze said. "Until we are ready."

Chirrut breathed, listened, felt. The echo-box was calm at his waist, and between its feedback and his own senses, he began to form an impression of the space. They were in the open, he knew, far out in the frigid desert, beneath the stars. He began to discern the larger shapes around them, the almost imperceptible slope of the ground beneath his feet, the thin sheen of sand blown across hard stone. He felt they were in a very old place, an ancient place, as old as the Temple of the Kyber or older, perhaps. He felt as if there were memories buried all around them, and stories, and that if he had a hundred years or a thousand to sit and listen, he might learn them.

He tapped his walking stick hard, once, on the ground, and started forward. Baze moved to follow him.

* * *

The path wound down, meandered, and beneath his feet Chirrut felt the skein of the sand and pebbles disturbed by their steps. Yet his footing remained sure, and he was not worried. This was not the first time he and Baze had been outside of the Holy City, and the desert of Jedha was familiar enough, even if it was not as well-known to him as the paths of their home. Still, for all his occasional journeys off the mesa, this place was new to him, and he was certain he had never visited it before in his life.

He had the impression of being watched, and part of him knew that this was certainly because either Tenza or Fortuna or another, or even several others, was doing just that. But it was more than that, too, not a sense of surveillance but rather of being *observed*, as if some great, unknown presence watched their progress with only the most passing interest, the most restrained curiosity.

"What do you see?" he asked Baze.

"The old monuments," Baze said. "The Three Faces."

"Tell me about them."

Baze grunted. "The desert has eaten at their features. One is a man, I think human. Another, I cannot tell, but from what remains of the body, perhaps a woman. The other a species I do not know. Perhaps Duros, once upon a time, before the sand and the wind did their duty."

"Do they face us?"

Baze hesitated ever so slightly, then said, "They surround us, Chirrut."

The temperature dipped yet again, and Chirrut knew they had passed into some deeper shadow cast by one of the enormous, ancient carvings. The path turned steep for another twenty paces, then abruptly leveled, and both the echo-box and his own hearing, his own sense of space and his place in it, told him they were now where they were meant to be, in some canyon between these forgotten monuments, surrounded and yet in the open.

Someone was there, waiting for them. Chirrut could feel him as certainly as he could feel the walking stick in his hand.

"What does he look like?" he asked Baze.

"I do not see anyone."

Chirrut pointed with the walking stick. An instant later, he heard Baze's movement, imagined him raising his new weapon.

"They take *everything*." The voice echoed off the stone around them, harsh, strained. A man's voice, full of pride and pain. "They take it *all*."

"Move where I can see you," Baze said.

"To give you a clean shot?" The voice seemed to choke for a moment, as if biting back a laugh. "That would be a mistake. You do not want to fire upon me."

"I will wait and see," Baze said.

Chirrut stepped forward, right across where he knew Baze was aiming.

"We come at your invitation," Chirrut said. "If this is an executioner's field, it is far too much effort spent on the likes of us."

"My invitation, yes." The man speaking seemed to consider this, then added, "Yes, that is true. We must be careful, you understand? We who fight them, we must always be careful."

"We understand."

The sound of movement bounced off the stone around him. A rasp, the drawing of a labored breath that made Chirrut think back to their meeting with Killi Gimm that morning—or, more precisely, the morning before—and the touch of her hand upon his. He tried to

find the speaker through the Force, reaching out for a sense of him, and what came back to him was an emptiness, a frame built of sadness and grief, filled with pain and rage and, deep within, an ember of light.

This man, whoever he was, had suffered horribly.

"Baze Malbus," the voice said off the stone around them. "Chirrut Îmwe."

"We know who we are," Baze said. "Who are you?"

The laugh again, not quite possessed of mirth. "Too difficult a question for a simple answer. Your friend would agree. Do you not agree?"

Chirrut smiled. "Perhaps, then, a name to start with?"

"Saw," the man said. "Saw Gerrera."

"If the name is meant to be known to us, I apologize," Chirrut said. "It is new, at least to me."

"If it were better known, I could not be here. If you knew it, then our enemies would know it, as well."

"Our enemies?"

"You know of whom I speak. You both know. You fight them, in fits, in starts. You strike and fade. You know the enemy."

"We fight for our home," Baze said.

"Is that all?" Saw Gerrera asked. "I fight for more. I fight for the galaxy."

"Then you will find Jedha very limiting," Chirrut said.

"Not as limiting as you might think." More motion. He was coming closer. "We have to start somewhere. Now, we fight on Jedha."

"We have an insurgency already," Baze said. "For all the good it is doing. Thank you, no."

"We are not insurgents. We are partisans. We are a rebellion. I bring battle-hardened fighters. I bring experienced tacticians. I bring pilots, a squadron of them. I bring the means with which to fight back. I am inviting you, both of you, to join me in this."

Chirrut leaned forward on his walking stick. "That is very kind of you, but if you have accomplished all you say, and if you can do all you say, why do you need us?"

Now Saw Gerrera was close enough that Chirrut could feel his presence. He was moving slowly, speaking to Chirrut and Baze both, focusing on the one, then the other.

"Because you know Jedha," Gerrera said. "I have not approached you by chance. It has taken us months to move into position here, and that has given us months to prepare, to learn. I have *learned* who you are. Four precision strikes against Imperial resupply convoys. You hurt them. Good. Together, we can do more."

"On Jedha," Chirrut said. "Why?"

"Where do we draw the line?" The man was speaking with a sudden intensity, now, a conviction that Chirrut imagined would be quite inspiring on the battlefield. "I saw Onderon fall beneath the Imperial flag. Countless other worlds. Innocent lives destroyed. Freedom stolen. Faith destroyed. Why not Jedha, in a city so holy to so many? What better place?"

Chirrut felt Baze responding to Gerrera's words, felt the big man shifting beside him, resettling himself, shifting the blaster in his hands. *Passion answers to passion,* Chirrut thought, *and thus Baze answers to Saw Gerrera.* If Chirrut was honest with himself, he could feel it, as well. The opportunity to act on behalf of the righteous. The chance to strike back at the Empire.

It was almost enough to make Chirrut ignore his instinct, the acute sense that Saw Gerrera's war was not, perhaps, as altruistic as he made it sound. That there was more to his presence on Jedha than a straightforward desire to send the Empire packing.

"We will take the fight to them," Gerrera said. "I would have you with me when we do."

Chirrut said nothing. Baze, perhaps despite himself, said nothing. Gerrera's heavy footsteps turned, moving away.

"Consider my offer," Saw Gerrera told them.

Fortuna accompanied them back to the Holy City; the speeder was driven by the same pilot who had brought them out, or so Chirrut thought. It *felt* like the same pilot, at least.

When they parted company, Fortuna pressed a tiny metal tube into Chirrut's palm.

"That can be used to reach me," Fortuna told him. "If you use it, I will conclude that you have decided to join with us."

"That will be a reasonable conclusion," Chirrut said.

The speeder departed, and Chirrut followed Baze back into their home, the room they shared. Neither had spoken on the return journey, and now, alone, Chirrut knew that Baze's patience was nearly exhausted. To his credit, Baze waited until the door was closed and locked before speaking.

"You know what I think," Baze said.

"Oftentimes, yes."

He heard Baze chuckle. "And what do I think now, Chirrut?"

"You think that fighting alongside Saw Gerrera and his . . . partisans is better than not fighting at all. And you think the time to fight is upon us."

"The time to fight has been upon us for a while, now. We help one at a time, we help Killi and Kaya. You try to keep the faith and the traditions, and I try to keep you from becoming so lost in the spiritual that you forget the physical. But every day the Empire's shadow grows over all of us. Every day the suffering increases."

Chirrut said nothing.

"They are killing us. Some of us faster than others. But they mean to take every last one of us before they go."

"But they will go," Chirrut said.

"Only when there is nothing left for them to take. And they will leave us with little, they will leave us with nothing."

"But they will leave."

He heard Baze sigh.

"The gun, my new gun," Baze said. "I found it at Denic's. It was part of the shipment we stole. It was meant for the stormtroopers. This weapon, Chirrut, it's a support weapon. It's supposed to hook into a vehicle's power and coolant systems. It's *that* kind of firepower. It fires thousands and thousands of bolts. I couldn't understand why the stormtroopers would need it. On a battlefield, yes, that would make sense. But here? In the city? Why would they need this firepower on one of their vehicles *here*?"

"They would need it if they knew about Saw Gerrera's partisans."

"Do you really think, if they knew about Gerrera's partisans, they would allow them even the smallest foothold on Jedha?"

Chirrut thought, shook his head slightly.

"So not for the battlefield," Baze said. "I asked Denic. Why this gun? Why do they need *this* gun? You will not like her answer. She said, 'Crowd control,' Chirrut. And the more I think about it, the more I think Denic is right. The Empire doesn't care about a single life in this city, not a single soul on Jedha. The fight is *here*, Chirrut. It is on us, and we must enter it."

"With Saw Gerrera."

"We stand a better chance with him than alone."

"If he is all he says he is."

That stopped Baze, at least for a moment.

"You think he was lying to us?" Baze asked.

"By omission rather than declaration," Chirrut said. "How did he seem to you?"

"In pain. Cautious. Hunted. Cunning."

"Did he have the face of a killer?"

Baze again paused. "He is no stranger to death."

"Did *you* trust him?"

"No," Baze said. "But I did *believe* him."

Chirrut sighed.

"Yes," he said. "Sadly, so did I."

From this moment I step into my next.

From this place I step into my next.

From this life I step into my next.

For I am one with the Force,

For ever and For ever.

—Coxixian Prayer for the Departed
From *Collected Poems, Prayers, and Meditations on the Force*,
Edited by Kozem Pel, Disciple of the Whills

CHAPTER 6

THE DOOR to the orphanage had been blown open.

It was a sliding door, two panels that came together at a midpoint, as was common in much of the Holy City. Its heavy metal construction had been designed to resist the elements, its paint long since worn away by the sand that blew through the city. Now, in addition to its weathered and scrubbed surface, a black scorch mark marred its center. The metal had bowed inward from the force of the blast, wrenching the door out of its track. Someone had tried to reset it, but the result was that one panel seemed to be about to tip over, top-heavy, and the other was tilted backward and crooked.

Baze looked at Chirrut. Sometimes, his friend would ask what he was seeing, how something looked. When he had first started doing so, Baze had presumed

Chirrut did this because, being blind, he wanted the use of Baze's eyes, for lack of a better phrase. But it hadn't taken Baze long to realize that this wasn't why Chirrut was asking at all. He didn't want to know what Baze saw, not literally; Chirrut wanted Baze's *impression*. If Chirrut asked, *What does the service droid look like?* he didn't want Baze to say that the machine was a meter and a half tall, or half a meter wide, and covered in laminate with scratches along its torso. What Chirrut wanted was for Baze to say that the droid was friendly, or past its sell-by date, or had seen better days, or looked like it was fresh off the assembly line. Chirrut wanted the perception *as Baze saw it*, and thus, in a way, he was asking for Baze's opinion.

Right now, Chirrut was frowning, head down.

"How does it look?" he asked.

"Not," Baze said, "good."

Chirrut shuffled forward a half step, held out one hand, feeling along the plane of the broken door. His fingers found the gap between the panels, traced the edge where the space opened. He leaned forward farther, moving closer to the opening.

"Killi Gimm!" Chirrut called. "Kaya Gimm!"

They heard no response.

Baze checked over his shoulder, looking up and down the narrow street. It was very quiet, though that was not to be mistaken for deserted. Movement in the surrounding buildings, shadows at windows. He looked along the street again. Too narrow for any of the standard Imperial GAVs or an AT-DP to make its way down. This would've been a detachment of stormtroopers either on specific assignment or perhaps on some sort of patrol, but already his instinct told him it was the former and not the latter. Maybe a half dozen of them, and this the only door damaged along the street. They'd known where they were going, Baze thought.

"We need to get inside," Chirrut said.

Baze grunted, shifted his new blaster cannon from his hands to its holster on his back, beside the coolant tank. He stepped forward as Chirrut stepped back, giving him room, and took hold of each of the panels through the gap. The metal was cold against his palms, and he could feel where the door had puckered with the blast against it, the way the surface bit at his skin like tiny teeth. He grunted again, louder, trying to pry the door open, then shifted his footing and tried the left-hand panel exclusively. It moved, grudgingly, and he leaned into it even harder, heard the metal grinding against the frame, against the sand, until it gave with a sudden snap of broken cable.

Chirrut ducked beneath his arm and turned sideways, slipped through the newly created opening. Baze wiped his hands on his pants, tried to follow him through the gap, and got hung up halfway through, as if someone had grabbed him from behind. He almost went for the cannon, then realized it was the cannon— or more precisely, the coolant tank—that had snagged. He backed out, ducked, tried again, and with some maneuvering got himself inside.

"They are not here," Chirrut said. He was standing in the middle of the common room, not moving.

Baze stepped past him. The room was much as he'd last seen it, minus the children and Kaya, of course. Chirrut sniffed at the air.

"No blasters," Chirrut said.

Baze grunted. He felt the weight of the weapon on his back, the coolant tank, the cannon. He felt, again, the strong desire to find someone to try it out on. He felt, in particular, that stormtroopers would be the ideal choice for this.

"I'll look around," Baze said.

"They are not here," Chirrut repeated. "And we already know what happened."

"I'll make certain."

"Check the kitchen first."

Baze grunted once again, then went off to check the kitchen first.

Stormtroopers were waiting for them when they emerged from the orphanage.

"You there," said the one at the front of the group. "Stop."

Chirrut, who had been leading the way back onto the narrow street, did as ordered. At the same time, his shoulders dropped and seemed to grow more rounded, his head drooped, and a smile appeared on his face that managed to appear both innocent and simple at the same time. Baze stepped through the broken doorway behind him, shifting to the right, keeping his hands at his sides where the stormtroopers could see them. There were five of them, including their leader. None of the troopers had their blasters raised, though they of course all had them in hand, and Baze took this to mean that they weren't looking to shoot them *right that moment*, but would maybe wait until they were certain they had a reason to do so. If he went for his cannon, that would change.

Baze adjusted his position slightly, keeping his back to the wall, careful not to scrape the coolant tank against the stonework. People went armed all the time throughout the Holy City, had done so even before the Empire's arrival, and carrying a weapon wasn't—in and of itself—an issue. But he had no idea if any of the troopers in front of them at this moment might recognize the Morellian blaster cannon that Baze now considered right and truly to be his own, nor if, upon recognizing it, they might wonder where he'd acquired it or even want it back.

He had no intention of giving it back.

"Yes?" Chirrut said. "And who are you, please?"

"He's blind," Baze explained to the armored soldiers in front of them. He said this patiently, as if he often had to excuse Chirrut's clumsiness and awkwardness to new people. "They're stormtroopers, my friend."

"Oh!" Chirrut straightened slightly, but his smile remained as it was. He had his walking stick planted in front of him, his left hand on the cap, right hand on the upper part of the staff, and now he raised it high and lifted his voice with it. "Imperial stormtroopers! You bring order to the disordered! Long live the Emperor!"

Baze kept half an eye on the walking stick as Chirrut brought it back to the ground, or more specifically, on his friend's grip on the stick. Chirrut could do a lot of damage with that staff if and when he so chose, and oftentimes the only warning Baze had that Chirrut was about to launch an attack with it was some subtle change in how he was holding it from one moment to the next. Judging by Chirrut's current grip on it, Baze figured things could go either way.

"What were you doing in there?" This was the lead, again. The pauldron on her right shoulder indicated that she was a sergeant.

"Where?" Chirrut asked. He sounded convincingly innocent.

"There. In there." She used an armored hand to indicate the broken door of the orphanage, then realized she was gesturing at a blind man and looked at Baze.

"Where?" Chirrut repeated.

"Several people saw you forcing your way into the building." The sergeant's voice crackled slightly through the speaker on her helmet. "We were standing right here when you came out. In there, the building, there."

"This building?" Chirrut reached back with his left hand, fingertips touching the stonework. He managed to look surprised.

"He gets confused," Baze told the sergeant.

"Fine," she said. "But you don't. What were you doing in there?"

Baze shrugged.

"Do you want us to take you in for questioning? Is that what you want?"

"No," Baze said. It was possibly the most sincere thing he'd said in weeks.

"Why's he dressed like that?"

"He's religious."

The sergeant muttered something that sounded to Baze like "another one of those." She sighed, her helmet speaker making her growing frustration all the more evident.

"The orphanage has been closed," the sergeant said.

"Ah," Chirrut said. "Where did they go?"

"Who?"

"The residents. The orphans. Those who cared for them. Where are they now?" He leaned forward on his stick slightly, tilting his head, as if hoping that by moving closer he might better hear her answer. His hands hadn't moved on the walking stick. "Did you arrest them? Are they guests of the Empire?"

"How should I know?"

"So that would mean you did not?"

"I said I don't know. Why would we arrest orphans? We're not monsters."

The sergeant's frustration was growing. Baze understood this. In his experience, Chirrut could be a tremendously frustrating person when he chose to be, and often enough, even when he didn't.

"The building was cleared out this morning after the raid," she continued. "Possession of stolen Imperial property. You know anything about that?"

The blaster cannon on Baze's back felt distinctly and suddenly heavier. Chirrut's left palm turned slightly, cupping the cap of his walking stick. His right hand dropped perhaps a centimeter lower down the shaft, an almost imperceptible adjustment that Baze was sure the stormtroopers had missed entirely.

"Is the street empty?" Chirrut asked.

"What?" said the sergeant.

"Empty enough," Baze told Chirrut.

"I thought so, but I wanted to be certain," Chirrut

said, and the smile vanished, and the walking stick came up and connected with the chin of the sergeant's helmet with a crack like a board splitting in two. Her helmet snapped back and she dropped at once, as if her legs had suddenly turned to air. The stormtroopers behind her were so stunned that Baze had pulled the cannon from its rig on his back and up to his shoulder before they'd even begun to move in response.

"Left," Baze said, and Chirrut swept his walking stick left, following in its arc and clearing the field of fire for Baze. Baze pulled the trigger, and two of the stormtroopers fell where they stood, but the remaining two caught the shots high in their torso, and the blasts sent both of them tumbling back, helmets over heels, until they cracked into the wall on the opposite side of the street before slumping, motionless, to the ground. Smoke wafted from where they'd been shot.

Chirrut straightened, smoothing the front of his robes as if nothing had happened.

Baze looked at the weapon in his hands.

"Yeah," he said. "This'll work."

It was evening and turning cold before they found Killi and Kaya and the children. The Holy City was a maze of streets, of neighborhoods, some of them hundreds, some of them thousands, and some of them—if you believed all the myths—hundreds of thousands of years old. It was a city made for hiding as much as it was a city built upon self-discovery. Once Baze and Chirrut had been assured that neither of the Gimms nor any of the orphans had been taken into custody, it was simply a matter of checking, in turn, the possible places they could have gone. But there were a lot of places, and the Holy City sprawled across the top of its mesa, and there were the stormtroopers to contend with.

They found them, finally, in the northwest part of the city, three and a half blocks from the Second Spire, a towering arrowhead of stonework that stabbed up at the sky like a needle. It was one of the tallest structures in the Holy City, and still it was only a third of the height of the Temple of the Kyber. The Second Spire—and the First, for that matter—had also been closed and sealed off by the Empire, but unlike the Temple of the Kyber, far fewer pilgrims made any attempt to visit it; the particular faith associated with the two towers was all but forgotten in the galaxy. The neighborhood, though still populated, was about as close to deserted as one could get in the Holy City, and traffic was far lighter.

The house had been abandoned some years earlier, shortly after the Imperial occupation had begun. Baze had been the one to discover it and pass it along to Chirrut to, in turn, pass along to Killi and Kaya as a potential site for a second orphanage should the need ever arise. It appeared as abandoned now as it had upon his initial discovery, and Baze keyed the old comm panel alongside the door expecting no answer and wondering where they would have to look next.

But the door opened, and Kaya stood there, in the old dark-blue mechanic's jumpsuit that she seemed always to wear, the tool belt slung low on her hips. Her hair fell in two long braids, draped over her shoulders and bound together just above her breastbone. Her eyes were blue, and red-rimmed from tears, and the skin beneath them had the sallow gray of fatigue and worry. Baze had always thought she was pretty—insofar as he thought such things about anyone at all anymore—but the relief he felt at seeing her was enough to make her seem positively radiant. He hadn't allowed himself to recognize just how worried he had been—for her, and her sister, and the children—until this moment.

"Baze," she started to say, but he stepped in and wrapped his arms around her and lifted her in a hug that took her off her feet. She stiffened for an instant, reflexively, surprised, and then all at once relaxed, and shuddered, her face against his chest. He felt her breath through his tunic as she let out a sob.

"I am sorry," Baze said. "We should have been there."

It was warmer inside the house, but not by much. In the time since it had been abandoned, others had come through the place and stripped it of almost everything of value, and that meant heating coils and faucet fixtures, everything that could be removed and sold. The bathroom was the only thing left marginally intact, though the door panel had been removed for whatever parts it could provide, which meant that it had to be opened and closed manually if anyone wanted privacy. There was almost no furniture. There was still power, and still running water, but the water was cold, and the power was pretty much useless as everything it might've powered had been stolen away.

Kaya had recomposed herself quickly. Baze knew she hated to worry or frighten the children, and that distress on her part would have precisely that effect, so she was hiding it. But he had seen her fear and her pain, and it nudged the simmering anger inside of him that much closer to a boil.

Kaya brought them to Killi, who was watching over the children with the help of the CZ droid. The children were still clearly upset, though quietly so, and Baze saw them tense, even flinch, at every loud noise from the street. A couple of the oldest orphans were still trying to console and soothe several of the youngest.

Killi was wearing her filtering mask around her neck, and her voice was hoarse when she spoke. She would use one hand to put the mask to her face to take a breath or two every couple of minutes. She left the CZ droid with the children, and the four of them moved to the kitchen, where they sat on the floor. Baze removed the harness and tank for the cannon and leaned back against the wall, Kaya beside him, while Killi and Chirrut sat in almost identical postures, their backs straight, cross-legged, facing one another.

"This is our fault," Baze said. "We brought this on you."

Killi shook her head. The mask was down, and her face was lined with worry, and like her sister, her eyes had the same sunken, almost hollow appearance. Her hood was down, as well, and her hair, cut short, was shot through with gray.

"We do not blame ourselves for the choices of others," Killi said. "The stormtroopers did what storm-troopers must do. We did what we must do. And you did what you must do."

Baze shook his head.

"Your heart demanded you help us."

"There was always a risk this would happen," Kaya said. "It could have been much worse."

"Was anyone hurt?" Chirrut asked.

"They pushed Killi to the floor." Kaya spoke before her sister could. "That frightened the children. B'asia hid under her bed, and one of the troopers was . . . unkind in getting her out, would not let Killi or me help. He grabbed her. She's Togruta, and he took hold of her by her montrals, and she screamed and tried to escape him and . . . he struck her."

"The stormtrooper struck a child?" Baze almost growled.

"She will be fine. At least the injury is not permanent."

Baze looked to Chirrut, and he knew that Chirrut was aware of his gaze, and he knew that Chirrut also knew what he was thinking. But Chirrut only said, "They took everything, yes?"

"All of it," Kaya said. "They accused us of stealing it ourselves, but I think even they knew that was absurd, which is why they didn't arrest anyone. We took only what we could grab before they kicked us out."

"I am worried it will get cold tonight," Chirrut said. "You will need blankets, heating coils, never mind food and water."

"I have contacted Gavra Ubrento at her shop. She has promised what she can spare, but it is not much."

Baze continued looking at Chirrut. It was petulant, he supposed, but he knew Chirrut could tell he was doing it. Gavra Ubrento worked as a roving mechanic, and had done business—and thus forged a loose friendship—with Kaya. But whatever Gavra could supply would hardly be enough.

There was a silence. From the other rooms, they could hear the CZ and the children; low voices, soft voices, even the droid's modulated vocoder. It was dark outside, and the darkness inside heavier as a result, and the few remaining working light fixtures cast small pockets of illumination that failed to lift the growing gloom.

"If you will excuse us for a moment?" Chirrut said. "Baze has something he wants to say to me alone."

Baze continued to stare at Chirrut. Killi and Kaya left the room without a word. The door slid back into place, and still Baze didn't speak, and neither did Chirrut. They sat in the growing darkness, listening to the faint sounds of the orphans and the two women who had taken it upon themselves to care for them, and to the sound of the old, battered droid that Kaya Gimm kept operational to help them. They sat, and the silence grew, and Baze imagined he could feel the movement of the Holy City settling into yet another uneasy, frightened night. He could almost feel the very weight of the Imperial Star Destroyer parked in orbit above Jedha, and through that giant ship, the incredible pressure of the Galactic Empire behind it. For a moment, he felt a spasm of pure dread, and then it broke, and gave way to his anger.

But Baze didn't say anything. There was nothing he needed to say. Chirrut knew what he was thinking, and Chirrut knew why he was thinking it.

He realized that Chirrut's lips were moving, that his friend was repeating the first phrase of the mantra, over and over.

The Force is with me and I am one with the Force. The Force is with me and I am one with the Force. The Force is with me. . . .

The Force was with Chirrut. Baze knew that, believed it. Had seen it. There had been a time, once, when Baze had felt the Force with him, as well.

Not anymore.

Chirrut's lips stopped moving. He sighed. With his left hand, he reached into his robe and removed the slim metal cylinder that Beezer Fortuna had given him. He ran his fingertips over it, tracing the shape, feeling the edges, the activator switch. He sighed a second time and then held out the device for Baze.

"Food, water, and medicine for the orphans," Chirrut said. "Blankets, heating units, beds if they can find them. Tell them that if they will provide these things, we will fight alongside Saw Gerrera."

Baze made the call.

Peace is a lie. There is only Passion.

Through Passion I gain Strength.

Through Strength I gain Power.

Through Power I gain Victory.

Through Victory my chains are Broken.

The Force shall free me.

—The Code of the Sith, translated from Qotsisajak
From *Collected Poems, Prayers, and Meditations on the Force,*
Edited by Kozem Pel, Disciple of the Whills

CHAPTER 7

CHIRRUT COULD FEEL the AT-ST stomping down the Blessing Way.

He counted the steps. Seventeen to reach the intersection with the Square of Stars.

Sixteen. Fifteen.

He moved his walking stick, settled it so it stood between his knees where he sat. He rested his forehead against the cap of the staff, the cold metal of the crystal containment lamp doing little to soothe his headache. He was tired, and he was frustrated, and he thought that either or both would bother him less if Baze's reassuring presence were somewhere over his shoulder. But Baze was not there, and now that they had allied with Saw Gerrera, it was an absence that Chirrut had come to feel more and more frequently in the last two months.

Fourteen. Thirteen. Twelve.

Two months since allying with Saw Gerrera's partisans. Two months since Saw Gerrera had agreed, without the slightest hesitation, to provide Killi and Kaya and the children with anything they needed, anything he could spare.

Eleven. Ten. Nine. Eight.

Two months since the start of Saw Gerrera's campaign against the Empire. Two months since Chirrut and Baze—and it had mostly been Baze thus far—had taught Gerrera's partisans the back-alley paths of the Holy City. Two months since the Empire had learned that Jedha, while occupied, would not submit willingly, nor quietly, and had responded in kind.

The AT-DPs were gone. They had been lighter, quicker, used by the garrison for patrols and quick response. Now there were AT-STs, a purer manifestation of the Empire's military might. The AT-ST was a battlefield weapon, and its presence in the Holy City meant that, at least in one thing, Saw Gerrera and the Empire agreed.

The fight for Jedha was on.

Seven. Six.

The first attack had been planned by Gerrera himself, passed along by Fortuna, and executed by a handful of his partisans, plus Baze and Chirrut. But since then it had been Baze more than Chirrut who had found himself in the fight, and whether it was due to a perceived liability in Chirrut's blindness or something more, Chirrut did not know. He suspected it had less to do with his lack of eyesight than what it was he *could* perceive. He suspected that he made Saw Gerrera uncomfortable.

Five. Four.

Gerrera had many secrets. Even now, after two months of helping the partisans, neither Baze nor Chirrut had the first idea where outside of the city Gerrera was making his base. When they met with him in person—and that occurred less and less frequently now—it was invariably where they had encountered him the first time, in the shadow of the Three Faces. Whether this was because Gerrera still didn't entirely trust them with the location of his hideout or for another reason entirely, Chirrut did not know. If Saw

Gerrera was paranoid, Chirrut could hardly blame him. The Empire had every reason to want the man dead. Soon it would have yet another.

Three.

Every act, every action, had its effect, unintended and intended alike, Chirrut reflected. Fighting the Empire for what was needed to keep the orphans in Killi and Kaya's care safe and warm and fed had resulted in the loss of the orphanage, the loss of everything that Chirrut and Baze had acquired to that very end. For every insurgent who had struck at a stormtrooper, another stormtrooper arrived to strike back.

Two.

Whether Saw Gerrera's war against the Empire had changed this, or whether it had simply accelerated the inevitable escalation, was yet another thing Chirrut did not know. The weapon Baze now employed against the Empire with frightening accuracy and to devastating result had been intended for use on the inhabitants of the Holy City. That had been *before* Gerrera had arrived. Chirrut was certain that if the Imperials could get away with keeping only those residents required for working the kyber mines on Jedha and somehow get rid of everyone else on the moon, they would do so.

They'd had no respect for the lives here to begin with. Gerrera's war had not changed that.

The Empire had arrived with arrogance and contempt.

What Gerrera's war had done was to add anger to the mixture.

Innocents suffer when a bully turns angry, Chirrut thought.

One.

The last step, the sound of the AT-ST's heavy, metallic foot hitting the ground, barely audible above the noise of the street around him. Almost a kilometer away, and now the walker was at the intersection of the Blessing Way and the Square of Stars, and Chirrut could almost feel the squads of stormtroopers accompanying it, could almost feel the presence of the laden haulers moving their cargo from the mines. And he could, without doubt, feel the presence of the kyber crystals, even from that distance, and he knew that there had to be many of them in this delivery, and that the crystals that had been mined were large ones, vibrant in the Force.

He keyed his comlink and said, "Now."

There was a click, then the staccato cluck and gurgle of one of Gerrera's men, the Tognath named Benthic.

Chirrut closed his eyes, felt the vibrations of the world around him rising up through the walking stick, pressing against his forehead.

He felt, then heard, the explosion.

He felt, then heard, the walker falling to the ground.

And now, he knew, the ambush was being sprung, an ambush that the Empire had no way to know was coming, because there had been no way to anticipate it. None of Saw Gerrera's partisans, nor Baze with them, would have been even remotely visible as they waited in the alleys and on the balconies all around the Square of Stars. None of them had been exposed, not even for a moment, not even to catch a glimpse of the approaching convoy. The stormtroopers would have been looking, and they would have seen nothing, because there had been nobody looking back at them.

Because the partisans didn't need to see. Because they had Chirrut, a kilometer away, feeling the ground shaking, waiting, counting, sensing for the right moment.

The ambush would be merciless, Chirrut knew. Gerrera's partisans took prisoners for one reason only, and none of the stormtroopers transporting this shipment had any intelligence value, so none would be taken alive. Right now, at this moment, stormtroopers were being cut down. Right now, at this moment, storm troopers were dying. Chirrut had done this, had made this happen. It had been a choice, the way allying with Gerrera had been a choice. And as with allying with Gerrera, it had been a choice made out of necessity.

There was no mercy to be found in this conflict, Chirrut knew. Not on either side.

The Empire would, once more, make the Holy City pay.

The first time, things went remarkably well.

Gerrera's only desire at that time, or so it had seemed, was much the same as Baze and Chirrut's—to strike at the Imperial occupation, to hurt the Empire. To this end, they had looked for the points of vulnerability in the occupation, and it had been Fortuna who had directed their attention to the mining operations at Gerrera's request.

"This is why they are here," Fortuna said. In the absence of Gerrera himself, it was Fortuna who appeared to handle operational planning. "Everything else is incidental. The closing of the temples, the restrictions on worship, all of that is ideological. Their *material* want is the kyber, and denying them the crystals will hurt them the most."

They had met in one of the tapcafes near the Old Shadows after hours, and it was crowded and noisy, and that made talking plans—somewhat paradoxically—easier than trying to find a secluded spot to whisper in the dark. Here, the noise and the bustle made them ordinary, unremarkable, and unworthy of notice. Instead of Tenza, this time Fortuna brought someone new, a male Meftian named Kullbee Sperado. Chirrut could sense Sperado even before he and Fortuna arrived, could feel the churning cold left in his wake, the way it clung to him.

"You are weighed by your past," Chirrut told Sperado when they were introduced. "You cannot outrun it."

The Meftian was silent long enough that Chirrut wondered if his insight had been mistaken, or if it had been too precise.

"He does that," Baze said.

"Do not apologize for me," Chirrut told him.

The Meftian reached out for Chirrut's hand, took it in one of his heavily furred paws. Chirrut could feel the rough texture of the man's flesh in the gaps of his fur.

"Will you pray for me?" Sperado asked.

"No," Chirrut told him. "But I will show you how to pray for yourself."

Sperado's grip tightened, and Chirrut felt the cold surrounding the Meftian dissipate for a moment. In that moment there was an instant's warmth, and he felt the man's hope.

"The mines," Fortuna said.

"The mines themselves?" Baze asked. "Or what comes out of them?"

"We do not have an actionable plan to assault the mines. Even explosives closing the mouth of the mines would only delay the operation for a few days, a week at the most."

"It would also claim the lives of more miners than stormtroopers," Chirrut said.

Fortuna continued on as if he hadn't heard either the criticism or the concern. "And while that would delay their mining operation, it would be a minor delay. What I propose is a quick hit on one of the speeder runs from the mines into the city, before they offload the crystals for transport off the moon."

"That could work," Baze said. "There are at least a dozen places along the route where it could be done easily."

"Would he come with us?"

Chirrut grinned. "Yes," he told Fortuna. "He, meaning me, would."

"I don't mean to offend, but you're blind."

Chirrut put a hand up in front of his face, waved it back and forth, gasped.

"Baze Malbus," he said. "Why didn't you tell me?"

Baze laughed. Fortuna didn't.

"Don't mistake his lack of eyesight for a lack of vision," Baze said.

The meeting ended shortly thereafter, and Chirrut walked with Sperado to the Old Shadows, as promised.

"I was on Serralonis," Sperado said. "When I was recruited."

"I do not know the world."

"Just a place."

"We all have a place."

Sperado thought about that, then asked, "If you lose that place?"

"You cannot lose what is inside you," Chirrut said.

"You can only misplace it. The task, then, is to find it again."

Angber Trel was attending to pilgrims in the Old Shadows when they arrived, and Chirrut made introductions, then departed. When he encountered Sperado again the next day as they prepared to attack the shipment from the mines, he asked if the visit had been of any help.

"Still looking for my place," Sperado told him.

Chirrut wished him luck.

They traveled outside of the city, using a speeder that Fortuna brought. There were another two of Gerrera's partisans with them, a Talpini and a human male. No one spoke. Fortuna held back as they took position, and once again questioned whether or not Chirrut's presence was required. Baze was annoyed.

"Wait and see," he said.

The route from the mine was through a narrow ravine, and Chirrut took position with Baze along one side of the cliff while Sperado, the Talpini, and the human took up a position on the other side. Chirrut had brought his lightbow, the one he had built himself as part of his training as a Guardian, and settled down amid the rocks before he snapped it open and ran his hands along the polished wood and the inlaid circuitry. It was at once as familiar in his hands as ever it had been, even though it had been years since he'd had cause to use it. He activated the impeller on the vambrace he wore on his left forearm, then relaxed as best he could into the moment. Baze powered up his cannon.

"How is that working for you so far?" Chirrut asked.

"I am trying something new," Baze said. "I can overcharge single shots. It will be enough to take down the speeder."

"Effective."

"It may not work. Which could be a problem."

"Because the speeder will get away?"

"Because the cannon may explode in my hands."

"I think I am going to find another place to wait," Chirrut said, half-heartedly starting to rise. Baze put a hand on his elbow and sat him back down.

Fortuna's voice came over their comlink. "Incoming."

Baze shifted forward, and Chirrut heard a clack from his cannon, the sound of his friend preparing to take his shot. Chirrut pulled a deep breath through his nose, released it past his lips, bringing the lightbow up in his hands. He felt the terrain spreading around them, a sensation of vertigo as he perceived the rise and fall of the desert as it narrowed to the ravine, and into the ravine the thrum of the speeder, riding low on its repulsor field, laden down with kyber crystals that seemed to glow in Chirrut's mind.

"Now," Fortuna said over the comlink.

There was a snap of explosives, the Talpini detonating the device he had planted, and rock tumbled from the edges of the ravine, and beneath them Chirrut felt the speeder swerve and he heard Baze fire the cannon. The thrum of the repulsor stopped, and the sound of metal shearing climbed up the walls of the ravine. Chirrut could feel the shape of the world in front of him, below him, where the natural terrain was broken by the presence of the machine, where the stone was disrupted by the living. Shots echoed from opposite their position, and Chirrut knew Sperado had fired, and so had the human, and that Sperado had hit and the human had not, and that there was a stormtrooper in the back of the vehicle raising a weapon onto his shoulder, and Chirrut knew what the stormtrooper wished to do. He adjusted his aim and fired, and the lightbow hummed a note to him, and he felt the bolt flying true, and he felt the stormtrooper drop.

Fortuna brought their speeder in, and they unloaded from the disabled one onto theirs, and they raced back to the edges of the mesa. Chirrut and Baze got out.

Before Fortuna raced away to take himself and the other partisans and their cargo to safety, he said, "Chirrut."

"Hmm?"

"My apologies for doubting you."

"It's all right," Chirrut said. "I *am* blind, after all."

Almost two months later, now, and more operations to vex and wound and enrage the Empire than Chirrut could count.

"It went well today," Baze said. "They barely had time to react, let alone return fire. It was over in less than two minutes. We took nearly thirty kilos of crystals back from them."

"Back to where?"

"Gerrera's people took them."

"So he is collecting them?"

"Only to keep them out of the hands of the Empire."

"And what does he do with them?"

"I have no idea."

Chirrut settled his walking stick across his lap,

smoothed out his sleeves. They were back in their room, and he could feel where Baze was working at the tiny stove, feel it when Baze paused in cooking their dinner to glare at him.

"Were there any injuries?" Chirrut asked.

"On our side? None."

"I meant the civilians."

"I know that's what you meant. 'Our side,' I said. Which means Jedha's side. No, no one was hurt."

"Save for the Imperials."

"If the Imperials do not wish to lose their lives," Baze said. "They are free to leave our home at any time."

"Yet they remain."

"Then we need to be more persuasive in our encouragement."

Chirrut laughed, unamused. A pot clattered on the stove, and he could hear the whine of one of the heating coils protesting as Baze coaxed it to life.

"What?" Baze asked.

"Do you not think that some hundred stormtrooper lives and some hundreds of kilos of kyber crystals denied them would send the message already?" Chirrut answered. "Do you not think that the message has been sent dozens of times with greater and greater clarity since Gerrera arrived, and that perhaps it is not being received as we wish?"

"If you have another way to get them to leave our home, I would love for you to share it."

"I do not know how to get them to leave our home, Baze. I only know that this method does not seem to be working. And that the wrong people are suffering for our actions."

There was another clatter from the stove—Baze setting something down or, more likely, slamming something down.

"Killi and Kaya, the orphanage, they are fine, they are safe. We saw it when we visited this morning. They gave us some more of that cursed Tarine tea. Gerrera has done as we've asked."

Chirrut just shook his head. Baze went quiet, finished preparing their meal, then set the bowl down in front of Chirrut before sitting heavily opposite him to dig into his own. Chirrut ate, chewing slowly. It was a noodle stew, with cut-up chunks of one of the many species of worms that lived in the sands, for added protein. It tasted bland, and the vendor, Sesquifian, hadn't done a particularly good job of cleaning the worms out before offering them to Baze. As a result, every fifth bite or so Chirrut would hear the crunch of a grain of sand between his teeth.

"How is it?" Baze asked.

"Perfectly wretched."

"You're welcome."

"Ah, yes, I meant, 'Thank you for making this meal for us, Baze.'"

Baze grunted, slurped at his broth. There was a pause, and then he said, "You're right."

"Hmm?"

"It is perfectly wretched. Sesquifian must've bought the worms from Dobias. What do you mean the wrong people?"

Chirrut set the bowl aside. "The Empire is compelled to respond."

"They are not compelled to do anything, Chirrut. No one made them invade our home, or close the temples, or occupy our world."

"But they have all the same. They are here, and now they take the kyber. And when we act to keep them from acquiring it, what do they do? They punish Jedha. Not Gerrera, not his partisans, not you or me, but *Jedha*."

Baze grunted.

"When we were at the orphanage this morning, did you count the children?" Chirrut asked.

"Twenty-two."

"So you did."

"I just said. Twenty-two."

"I heard twenty-four. Double the number of children in their care before Gerrera's campaign began. Twelve more children who have lost their parents either to the Empire or to the partisans perhaps not being as careful as they could be in their attacks."

"So you would blame Gerrera?"

"No," Chirrut said. "No more than I would blame you or me for the violence the Empire brings. But it is as Killi said all those months ago. We have entered a cycle, do you not feel it? At first we struck at the patrols. Then we struck at the convoys. Now we strike at the shipments. First the stormtroopers established check-points. Then they want scandocs and have patrols on the streets. Now? Now they will stop and search any-one they do not like the looks of, and if you dare resist, they beat you, and if you try to flee, they shoot you. Where does this escalation end, Baze?"

Baze didn't answer. Chirrut heard him rise, heard him gathering the bowls, moving to clean up after the meal. Perhaps there was nothing to say, or more accurately, nothing Baze could say. Chirrut himself had been wrestling with this very question for weeks now. The fact was simple, and one didn't need working eyesight to recognize it: Gerrera's arrival on Jedha had made a bad situation worse.

Before, there had been scattered insurgents, any affiliation between them loose at best. There was no coordination, and to be honest, very little in the way of tactics or even skill. But one of the things Chirrut had understood after their initial meeting with Tenza and Fortuna two months prior was that he and Baze were not the only people to whom Gerrera had made overtures. The man had done his homework; he had sent agents to Jedha before his arrival, had done so far enough in advance that when he arrived, those agents had been able to present him with fairly accurate intelligence as to who might be worth recruiting and who might not.

The result was that there were few independent insurgents left in the Holy City. One way or another, if a sentient wielded a weapon against the Empire, they were doing it on behalf of Saw Gerrera. Suddenly, attacks that the Empire had clearly deemed merely a nuisance, the cost of doing business, had become more expensive. Instead of the occasional resupply cache being hijacked, now whole cargo shipments were vanishing. Instead of an occasional potshot taken at a stormtrooper or officer, now attacks were coordinated, and the targets were growing ever more significant. LZ-Besh and LZ-Dorn had each been attacked in force; LZ-Besh had been abandoned as a result. Word was that over fifteen stormtroopers had died in the assault.

Chirrut thought of what Killi had said, that each does as they must. For the Empire, its must was to deploy walkers and combat assault tanks. To build checkpoints and crew them with heavy blaster emplacements. To search each and every starship that made landing at the port, and to increase the taxes on just about every import and export out of Jedha. To fly TIE fighters in patrols over the city, using them to coordinate the deployment of assault teams who would eliminate any pocket of resistance or base used by the insurgency they could find.

The refugee situation, already bad, was becoming intolerable. More and more people were going hungry. More and more people were becoming sick. More and more people were dying.

"I'll be back in a while," Baze said.

Chirrut reached for his walking stick. "Wherever you are going, I will come with you."

"No."

Chirrut hesitated, prepared to pull himself to his feet with the stick. He frowned. "You are going to meet with more of Gerrera's people."

"No," said Baze. "I am going to talk to Gerrera himself."

Those who set a course and cannot adjust their heading

will break upon the rocks as surely

as those who sail heedless of direction.

We cannot change the direction of the wind.

Nor can we afford to be blown whichever way it so chooses.

We act; we decide; and we are acted upon.

So it is in all things that I wish to honor those

who have come before.

So it is in all things that I wish to prepare the way

for those who shall come after.

And I remind myself:

in the Force, there is no end, but only beginnings.

—Oz Ladnod, Poet to the Royal Court of Onderon
From *Collected Poems, Prayers, and Meditations on the Force,*
Edited by Kozem Pel, Disciple of the Whills

THEY MET IN THE SHADOW of the Three Faces, as they had every time before. Baze heard him coming before he saw him, the heavy stride. Baze had been sitting on a boulder, staring at the sky and the glowing dot that was the Star Destroyer, still parked high in orbit. He stood when he heard Gerrera coming.

"Good work today," Gerrera said. "The Empire will feel it."

Baze thought of what Chirrut had said earlier that night. "All of Jedha will feel it."

"The Empire will do what they always do when they feel their control is slipping." Gerrera motioned to the boulder Baze had been using as a seat, moved to another nearby, and settled himself carefully, wincing slightly as he sat. "They will take more freedom, and they will punish more people. The result is the same. More and more people will rise to fight alongside us."

Baze had been waiting for long enough that his eyes had adjusted, and he was able to see Gerrera clearly despite the dark. They watched one another for several seconds without speaking, and Baze wondered how much of a reflection he was seeing. A vision of his future self, perhaps.

"I brought something," Saw Gerrera said. "Share a drink with me, Baze Malbus?"

"I will drink anything you offer," Baze said. "Except for Tarine tea."

"It's filthy stuff, isn't it?"

"You can still get chav tea at some of the tapcafes, but for some reason every time I'm offered tea, it's Tarine."

"I was offering something stronger." Gerrera reached back around his hip, unhooked a flask from his belt. He uncapped it, then offered it to Baze, who took it, sniffed, and sipped. Whatever it was stung his tongue and his throat, then opened into a blossom of warmth that sent the chill of the desert night fleeing. Baze returned the flask.

"Not Tarine." Gerrera smiled.

"No. What is it?"

Gerrera took a drink himself, made a slight face. "*Bahkahta*. It's an Onderon drink. I've had to learn how to brew it myself. This is not the best I've ever had, I admit. But my recipe is getting better."

"Hard to get?"

"Harder for me. Onderon was my home." He looked at the flask in his hand thoughtfully, then passed it back to Baze. "My home is gone."

"Onderon remains." Baze took another sip. The sting was softer this time, but the warmth more intense.

"The planet, yes. But our way of life is gone, our culture is gone, our beliefs are gone. That's what the Empire does. We were a republic that celebrated our differences, thousands and thousands of worlds, peoples, lifestyles. Not anymore. There is one Empire. Either you are part of it, or you are destroyed."

He took another drink from the flask.

"Think about it," Gerrera continued. "Think about stormtroopers."

"I try not to."

"They're meant to look the same, yes? Identical. Forget the variations in their duties or assignments. One looks like another. There's a genius to it. I take your son, your daughter, I put them in the armor, do you dare rise up? Would you shoot your brother? Your mother? You cannot know who is beneath the armor. Faceless. Or, rather, the face of the Empire. Expressionless. Almost featureless. Yet ominous. Join, and you are just another anonymous citizen, but you belong. And if you do not, you must be eliminated."

Gerrera offered the flask once more, and Baze took it. A piece of him wished that he had brought Chirrut to the meeting after all. He would have enjoyed the conversation, Baze thought. More, it would have allowed Chirrut an opportunity to learn more about Gerrera.

Baze took a swig, gestured with the flask at the desert around them. "This is hardly worth fighting over."

"They want the kyber."

"We didn't know that when they first arrived. Many thought their occupation would not last, or would be token. Most believed they had come because of the temples. We thought, they have come to crush belief, because belief leads to hope, and hope can topple monsters. They will stay long enough to crush hope, but they do not understand that hope can be a very small thing. It doesn't need much to survive. An occasional breath of air. A flicker of warmth. Hope can live in a vacuum."

"You sound like your friend."

"Only when he is not around." Baze grinned.

Gerrera leaned forward, taking the offered flask back. He was looking at Baze with a new curiosity. "So you have hope, still?"

Baze shrugged, spread his hands on his thighs. They were big hands, and he had done a lot of harm with them, and sometimes he wondered if his hands would not have been better used for gentler work—what it would have been like to have been a painter or sculptor or baker.

"I do not know what I have anymore," Baze said. "I have a home, and will fight for it. I have those I love, and I will fight for them. I see injustice, and will fight against it. I suppose these are the best reasons to fight."

The lines in Gerrera's face deepened, and his eyes drifted from Baze to a point past his shoulder, looking for something that perhaps wasn't there, or perhaps looking into memory. Then he tilted his head back, and Baze thought he had grown short of breath, would reach for the respirator mask he wore on the heavy body armor that encased his torso, but Gerrera did not. Instead, he was gazing up at the stars overhead.

"I have lost so much, so much," Saw Gerrera said

softly. "I have given so much, so much, to this fight. My hope is not all it once was."

He lowered his eyes back to Baze, rapped the knuckles of one fist against his chest.

"The Empire has hounded me across the galaxy. Planted spies within my cadre. They tried to assassinate me on Errimin, poisoned me with teccitin. I was sick for months. On Ghita there was a sniper who missed by centimeters. They sent an astromech droid laced with nanoexplosives, and it went off and killed four of my best people, and again I was wounded, but I survived. That time, Fortuna said to me, 'You are lucky. The Force is with you.'"

Baze grunted.

"I admire your friend Chirrut greatly, you know that?" Gerrera said, and he saw Baze's surprise and nodded, adding, "I do, I truly do."

"Why?"

"Because faith requires hope. The one thing your friend does not lack is faith."

"His faith has been tried."

"So has yours."

Baze said nothing.

Gerrera sighed, offered the flask a last time to Baze,

who raised a hand to indicate he'd had enough. Gerrera took a last sip, then replaced it on his belt.

"You did not wish to meet to share a drink and talk of our struggles," Gerrera said.

"No."

"So?"

"The orphanage."

"Is there a problem?"

"There are twenty-four children, now," Baze said. "There will be more."

"The result of the Empire's cruelty."

"Who made them orphans doesn't matter to me right now. What matters is how we can help them."

"I can try to arrange for more basic supplies, food and water, but we are already—"

"No, that doesn't solve the problem. It delays it."

"What, then?"

Baze told him what he was thinking, and Gerrera listened, frowning in concentration. When Baze had finished, Gerrera stared at him for the better part of a minute, considering, and then, finally, barked a sharp, short laugh.

"We can do that," Saw Gerrera told him.

Those who would see all the galaxy burn,

But themselves,

And who would see all the tears shed,

But their own,

Diminish and diminish and diminish,

Unto nothing,

And from nothing,

To nothing,

Is no thing.

—Mete Janvaren of Mirial
From *Collected Poems, Prayers, and Meditations on the Force,*
Edited by Kozem Pel, Disciple of the Whills

CHAPTER 9

THE NEXT DAY was a hard one for the Holy City.

It started as the sun was rising, a thunder that echoed from the desert floor and dropped from above all at once, and those who made it to their windows or were already outside looked up and froze in place, and stared. The Star Destroyer had broken orbit, had entered the atmosphere, and as they watched it came closer, and grew larger, and its shadow grew until it spread across the Holy City. The Star Destroyer descended, lower and lower, until some of those watching wondered if the massive vessel meant to simply crush them all.

Then it stopped, parking overhead, engines thrumming, and there was only that sound and nothing else, the Holy City holding its breath.

Then the skies began to scream with TIE fighters.

Now almost all of the Holy City was awake, and watching, staring at the display. It filled them with dread, and it filled them with fear, and that was, of course, precisely the point. As they watched, transport after transport dropped from the Star Destroyer's hangar bay, banked sharply, and then dived straight for the city. It was a combat deployment maneuver, executed rapidly, a display of skill and discipline that served as a reminder of what, exactly, the Empire could do should it put its mind to it.

Some of the transports made for the established LZs or the spaceport. Several ignored them altogether, diving for the city itself, pulling up sharply mere meters above the ground, barely avoiding crashing into buildings and people. Their rear doors lowered and before they had locked into position, the stormtroopers were on their way out, their E-11s at their shoulders, shouting orders. They secured their landing sites with speed and efficiency. Citizens of Jedha were given one warning to keep their distance. After that, they were shot.

The initial deployment took seventeen and a half minutes, from the time the screaming of the TIEs announced the start of the operation until the last of the troop transports returned to the safety of the Star Destroyer overhead. When it was done, the storm-trooper presence in the Holy City had quadrupled, and with them had come another eight AT-STs, ten AT-DPs, and six newly modified TX-225 assault tanks. Rumors began flying almost immediately that similar deployments had been made at the head of each kyber mine. Someone claimed that another Star Destroyer was on its way to join the one parked overhead, that it was entering the system even now. Several people reported seeing, with their own eyes, two ships shot from the skies as they tried to lift off from the Holy City's spaceport, even though each had previously secured the appropriate clearances.

This was only the first phase.

The stormtroopers moved through the city in their customary fire teams, four troopers to each team, but now with two teams working in tandem. The teams worked block to block, relentlessly, methodically. They stopped individuals at random, demanded documentation, conducted random searches and aggressive interrogations. Some of those detained were shown images from handheld holoprojectors, pictures of known or suspected insurgents or criminals. By noon, three of the more notorious criminal hotspots had been raided, resulting in firefights at two of them, with seven fatalities and three times as many injuries. Many of those suspected of being part of the insurgency were stunned outright, then placed in binders and loaded onto heavily armored Imperial Troop Transports, and the ITTs were then driven to the spaceport or the nearest landing zone, and the prisoners removed directly to the Star Destroyer overhead.

Then the partisans began to strike back.

The first firefights were minor, more skirmishes than protracted engagements, but they established the pattern. One or two of Gerrera's fighters would open fire from concealed positions, exposing themselves for the least amount of time possible, then quickly retreat. Stormtroopers would respond, call for reinforcements—a tank, or an AT-ST or AT-DP. As they did, another pocket of partisans would attack in another part of the city, and while the Empire responded, yet another attack would follow.

Sometimes, the stormtroopers would respond to find the partisans had already withdrawn. Sometimes, the stormtroopers would respond to find the partisans lying in wait, attacking from all sides. Sometimes, the stormtroopers would respond to find the street had been booby-trapped, their support vehicles targeted.

Four blocks south of LZ-Dorn, early in the afternoon, there was an explosion that could be heard all across the city. An acrid plume of black smoke rose from the site, and within minutes came the sounds of blaster fire, and of smaller detonations. The TIEs screamed in from above once again, flew so low they seemed to skim over the buildings, narrowly avoiding smashing themselves to pieces against the domed rooftops of several of the older temples. Moments later, three X-wing fighters were spotted coming in from the east, white with black markings. Nobody had ever seen them before; nobody had the first idea where they'd come from. As they engaged the TIEs overhead, new rumors began to fly that these were Saw Gerrera's pilots, that he had been holding them in reserve, that he had sent them in the Holy City's hour of need.

The X-wings took the TIEs by surprise, shot two down within seconds. People cheered. Then the cheers died as quickly as they had risen as one person after another on the ground looked to the Star Destroyer to see TIE after TIE dropping from the hangar bay. One TIE, then another, and another, and another, and another, until the numerical superiority was so over-whelming the streets went silent. One of the X-wings was turned to a ball of flame and debris, careening away to disintegrate over the desert. A second was hit beneath its fuselage, port side. It went into an uncon-trolled corkscrew that sheared its lower port S-foil clear off the fighter. The broken wing came crashing down near the Path of Judgments, smashing through the roofs of two of the homes there and killing one of the occupants. The fighter fought to right itself, its pilot somehow managing to crash just north of the Division Wall that separated part of the Old City from the New City, which was itself well over five thousand years old. Stormtroopers descended on the crash site immedi-ately, but the pilot seemed to have escaped the landing. They began an immediate search.

The remaining X-wing, realizing what everyone on the ground already knew—that the situation had turned from heroic to suicidal—went full evasive and fled toward the western horizon. The last anyone saw of it, there were six TIE fighters in pursuit. Some peo-ple claimed the pilot escaped. Others claimed that the pilot had been captured, along with the one who'd crashed outside the Division Wall. Even now, they said, both pilots were being interrogated aboard the Star Destroyer, and it was a certainty that one or the other would give up Saw Gerrera's hiding place, and that the partisan leader would soon be in custody, or dead, or both.

The battle on the ground continued for another hour or more. A new battery of rumors began to spread: Gerrera himself was in the city, and the Empire had him cornered. He and his partisans were fighting for their lives. Some, hearing this, returned to their homes, locked their doors, held close to their loved ones if they had loved ones to hold. A few others took their weapons and ran through the emptying streets in the hope of helping the partisans only to find stormtroopers ready for them. Most of those who went to fight ended up shot dead.

It was over before sunset. A fire had started during the battle, and the Empire made no attempt to put it out. Most of the Holy City's civil services had long ago ceased to exist in any useful or recognizable form, and there was no fire brigade to speak of, and the citizens who responded to try to fight the blaze quickly realized it was an exercise in futility. They had no running water and none of the specialized firefighting equipment the brigade once used, and the stormtroopers refused to help. In the end, people did the best they could to save one another and their few precious belongings, and then withdrew to let the fire burn itself out.

The glow of the flames lasted until well after nightfall.

Where you see darkness,

I see stars.

—Laech Min-Glsain
From *Collected Poems, Prayers, and Meditations on the Force*,
Edited by Kozem Pel, Disciple of the Whills

CHIRRUT CARRIED the boy through the streets in his arms, trying to assure him that everything would be all right.

"Say this with me," Chirrut said. "'The Force is with me, and I am one with the Force.'"

The boy said nothing. His name was Althin. He was a Rodian, and Chirrut could feel his long and slender fingers on his arm through the sleeve of his robe, his grip tight. The boy's other arm had been broken, was now bound to his chest with the sash from Chirrut's robe in a makeshift sling. If Chirrut was forced to move quickly to avoid the stormtroopers or a vehicle or even suspected partisans, and if he was not careful when he did it, the motion would jostle Althin. Then the boy would whimper, pain radiating through his broken limb, penetrating his shock and his numbness.

Althin was a week from his eighth year, and he was a good boy who loved to read and loved to draw, and once Chirrut had been in the market and heard a group of pilgrims arguing about how to find the Emitter of Constant Hope, and he had heard Althin introduce himself and give them directions, and when the pilgrims had offered to pay him in thanks, he had instead asked they give the money to someone who might need it more.

Chirrut knew all these things because he had known Althin since the day he was born, and he had known his parents even longer than that. Althin's parents had come to Jedha from Rodia before the end of the Clone Wars. They had bought a storefront one block off the Blessing Way and made their home above it. They had stayed in business selling guides and simple works on spirituality, the Force, and other such things primarily to the pilgrims and tourists who came to visit the Holy City. Their true passion had been ancient manuscripts, whether recorded on old data tapes or decaying discs or even, in the rarest of cases, books, all manner of older texts collected from all around the Outer Rim. Althin's mother, Steya, had a particular passion for martial arts, not solely its literature but also its practice. Shortly after settling in the Holy City, she had sought out Chirrut and asked him to teach her in zama-shiwo, one of Jedha's native fighting styles and one in which Chirrut had achieved a level of mastery. For several years Steya and Chirrut would meet in the morning outside the Temple of the Kyber to practice the forms. Althin's father, Tok, had no interest at all in esoteric fighting styles, but instead had been passionate about theater, in particular opera, and even more particularly, Bith opera from the Middle Era of the Old Republic.

Somewhere to his left, Chirrut felt the thrum of a heavy repulsorlift field, and a fraction later heard the sound of metal on metal, the grinding of gears. There was a lot of motion around him, the city had been in spasms all day, but since the fighting had broken out near LZ-Dorn it had grown much worse. He trusted to his senses, and failing those, to his echo-box, but after hours of moving through the city trying to give aid to those in need, he was tired, and it was beginning to tell on him. He pulled up abruptly, and the move caused Althin to whimper again.

"It's all right, little one," Chirrut told him. "It's all right, I have you."

Using the echo-box more than his memory, he stepped back, moved one hand from where he was cradling the boy, feeling for the wall, and finding it, feeling his way to the recess of a doorway. He stepped back into it, bringing his arm back to Althin, waiting. The tank was coming closer, rumbling, and Chirrut could taste the dust the vehicle set into the air. The stonework around them thrummed in sympathetic vibration with the repulsorfield.

"The Force is with me, and I am one with the Force," Chirrut told Althin. "And I fear nothing, for all is as the Force wills it."

Althin stayed still in his arms, silent once again.

And why does the Force will to take a child's parents? Chirrut found himself wondering.

For the first time in many, many years he felt a stab of deep, powerful anger in his breast. An anger so hot and so insistent and so surprising, it stole his breath. A young man's anger, familiar and all the more unwelcome because of that. An anger that had been lurking within him since dawn—since before dawn, if he was honest. An anger directed at everyone and everything, a fury at the injustices of the universe, but pointed at the Empire and Saw Gerrera specifically, and in equal measure.

The tank was passing, Chirrut could feel it, hear it, but for the moment he had no *sense* of it, no sense of who rode within or upon it. This had been the problem all day: the feeling that his connection to the Force, however tenuous it was at the best of times, had diminished or even broken. It had grown worse as he'd moved from crisis to crisis, as he'd found husbands mourning wives shot by stormtroopers in the streets, as he'd come upon wreckage and damage from a dozen smaller battles that had raged around the city in response to the Empire's own reprisals, and on, and on, and so it went. The cycle he had spoken of to Baze grew worse, exactly as predicted. That was the fighting at LZ-Dorn, he knew; the partisans had seen an opportunity to lash out at the Empire once more, and they had seized it.

Chirrut wondered if that was where Baze had gone. If his friend was dug in with Gerrera's partisans, pouring his fury out in the blaster fire directed at the newly arrived stormtroopers. He hadn't heard from Baze since he'd left their home the night before. Chirrut wasn't actually worried for his safety.

What he was, Chirrut suddenly understood, was angry at Baze, too.

"You there."

Most of all, though, Chirrut was angry at himself.

"You there, I'm talking to you."

That was it. He was angry at himself. But why, exactly? Because he felt guilty for what he had done, for his part in bringing about the violence, the reprisals of this day? No, the Empire needed to be fought. It had to be resisted. His faith held him to a moral code, but that morality was the same regardless of any faith in the Force. One did not need to believe in the Force to know right from wrong. Many who held no faith in the Force acted righteously, and he had known more than one sentient who had acted selfishly, even cruelly, and used belief to justify doing so.

"Step out of there."

Angry at himself because he felt powerless? This was closer to the truth. Angry at himself because he was one man, alone, and no matter what he did, it would not be enough. He could not end Jedha's suffering. He could not even, apparently, get one injured, grieving child to safety.

"What's the matter with you? Are you deaf?"

Angry at himself because he had been arrogant enough, perhaps, to believe he could.

His senses opened once more. He could feel the stormtrooper now, his presence, his motion. The tank had passed, come to a stop, and this stormtrooper had been riding outboard and had seen him and Althin. Now the tank was idling a few meters along the street, and the stormtrooper had come back to question them.

"Blind," Chirrut said. "Not deaf."

"What's going on here? Where are you taking that Rodian?"

"His arm is broken. I am taking him to get medical attention."

"Where are his parents?"

"They're dead."

He heard the stormtrooper's plastoid armor creak slightly, could imagine him shifting uneasily. Chirrut knew why, and he imagined that if he were more forgiving he would have told the stormtrooper that—just this once—the Empire was not responsible.

At least, not directly.

"You two need to clear the street," the stormtrooper said. "There's going to be a curfew in effect tonight. Anyone out without authorization will be shot."

"Thank you for the information."

The stormtrooper creaked again, moving away, and Chirrut heard him exchanging words with another, the clank of the tank's treads as the vehicle moved into gear and rolled away.

"The Force is with me, and I am with the Force," Chirrut told Althin.

The boy still did not answer him.

They continued on their way.

The smell of the smoke faded as they moved into the northwest quarter, and Chirrut's sense not only of where he was but of what was around him grew steadily with their progress. Twice more he and Althin were stopped by stormtroopers, and each time they were allowed to pass without incident, though in neither case was there the hint of empathy that Chirrut had found with the stormtrooper from the tank. Near the First Spire, they heard the sound of blaster fire, and Althin responded to that, tensing as Chirrut carried him. The boy had shifted in his arms, now with his good arm around

Chirrut's neck and his legs wrapped around Chirrut's waist. He still had yet to speak.

They reached the orphanage and Kaya let them inside, and without a word she took Althin from Chirrut's arms. The boy clung to Chirrut, reluctant to let go.

"I will not be far," Chirrut told him. "And Kaya knows how to make your arm stop hurting."

He felt the boy touch his face, the soft, suction-tipped ends of his fingers on his cheek like flower petals. Chirrut took the boy's hand in his own, giving it a squeeze that he hoped was as reassuring as it was gentle. Kaya carried him away, and Chirrut let his walking stick return to his hands, rolled his neck, loosening the muscles that had tensed and tightened during the long walk through the Holy City.

"Tea?" Baze asked.

Chirrut turned his head in surprise, orienting to the sound of his friend's voice.

"It's chav," Baze said. "Not that wretched Tarine stuff."

For a second, Chirrut found himself at an utter loss for words. He hadn't heard Baze's approach, and Baze was not, generally, a man who did things quietly. More, he hadn't *sensed* Baze's approach, nor even his presence, and if there was a presence that Chirrut Îmwe knew in the Force more than any other—more, perhaps, than his own place in it—it was that of Baze Malbus.

"Well, if it's chav," Chirrut said, "I can hardly refuse, can I?"

"You were worried about me," Baze said.

"I was growing concerned," Chirrut said. "But only because I missed your nagging."

Baze put the glass of tea into Chirrut's hands. "Althin's family?"

"Steya and Tok were killed when the partisans went after one of the AT-DPs," Chirrut said evenly. "From what I could gather, they set explosives along the street, and when they were triggered it brought down the walker along with several of the homes. They had been hiding inside from the fighting. Where they thought it would be safe."

He sipped his tea.

"Nowhere is safe," Baze said.

"Not anymore, no. When did you get here?"

"Before midday. I thought one of us should be here, in case the fighting reached this far. I knew you'd come here sooner or later."

"I thought you would be with the partisans."

"Not today."

They drank their tea. Killi came to check on them, returning Chirrut's sash.

"We've set the arm," she told him.

"Has he said anything?"

"No. He is in shock, Chirrut. Killi got him to take a couple of sips of juice, but he would not eat. She is with him and the children right now. Perhaps their company will do him good."

"What will do him good is love, peace, quiet, and time," Chirrut said.

"Of those, only the first is guaranteed."

"I know," Chirrut said. "But one of those is better than none, and that is why I brought him to you."

Killi began coughing. Chirrut heard Baze pouring more tea, and as the fit subsided, heard Killi thank him, then the sound of her drinking.

"Althin will not be the only child to become an orphan today," she said. "We are running out of room."

She finished her tea and left them. Chirrut listened to the door sliding closed after her, heard the children, the sound slipping through the open doorway as she went.

"She is right," Chirrut told Baze. "These walls will not be able to hold all of them much longer."

Baze said, "There is a solution."

"If this is the same solution, it does not—as I said before—seem to be working."

"No, a different solution."

"You have my attention."

"They leave."

Chirrut turned the glass in his hand. He could feel the precise line of heat marking the level of the tea. It was an idea that had simply not occurred to him. The idea of leaving Jedha had never occurred to him, and he knew for a fact that Baze would never abandon their home. They were a part of this world, a part of this city, and one of the blessings of living in this place was that the galaxy had always been willing to come to them, no matter how far or inconvenient the journey here might be.

"That," Chirrut said, "is an interesting solution."

"But a good one."

"I would not go that far. There are a number of problems with what you are proposing, Baze. You assume Killi and Kaya would be willing to leave Jedha. You assume we could acquire a ship for them. You assume that the Empire would let said ship depart. Then there is the question of where they would go."

"There are worlds the Empire has not yet reached."

"The operative word being 'yet.'"

Baze grunted. It was his annoyed grunt. "It is not a question of escaping the Empire. It is a question of escaping *here*, Chirrut."

"And hoping."

"Yes."

"Have you talked to Killi or Kaya about this?"

"I wanted to talk to you first."

"There are still many problems."

"Fewer than you might think," Baze said. "Saw Gerrera has agreed to help us get a ship."

The moment between breaths

Is the balance of the Force.

Between life and death.

Rest and action.

Serenity and passion.

Hope and despair.

—Nartun Trecim, Ascendant of Mau
From *Collected Poems, Prayers, and Meditations on the Force*,
Edited by Kozem Pel, Disciple of the Whills

THERE WAS A CANTINA at the spaceport, but it wasn't doing much business anymore, because nobody wanted to linger there. Traffic in and out could run from a steady flow to a trickle, but even at its most active it was a far cry from what the Holy City had been used to before the Imperial occupation. Now, if a ship set down, it did so with a mind to get in and out as quickly as possible. Whether delivering goods or taking pilgrims back to their homes, it was much the same. Land, unload, refuel, and go, all of which could be accomplished in under an hour if things were favorable.

Things were rarely favorable these days, mostly because all arriving and departing ships were subject to search by Imperial authorities. This meant passengers and crew were questioned, scandocs verified, and if anything at all appeared less than aboveboard, a scanning crew was dispatched to find out the who and the why of it all. Given all that, it was hardly a surprise that passengers and crew alike had no interest in lingering over a drink or a meal.

The only ships that weren't subjected to such intense scrutiny were, of course, ships dispatched to Jedha by the Empire. Imperial transports were given a cursory scan, logged, and provided all the computers agreed that the ship was where it should be at roughly the time it was expected to be there, that was that. The Empire was free to go about its business.

The cantina was built along the spaceport promenade, facing the long line of landing bays, most of which had their doors open. Windows ran along the wall to give patrons a view of the passersby, or to give the passersby a view of the patrons, depending on where you were when you looked.

Baze sat in the second booth down from the entrance, with a view from his window directly onto bay eighteen. He wore his customary body armor but had draped a dust shroud over his shoulder and wrapped it around himself, attire more appropriate to any number of pilgrims who might be waiting for a ride back home. The Morellian cannon and its coolant tank had been placed in a container that now rested beside his knee. It was a little overlarge for a pilgrim's luggage, but Baze was considered by many to be a little overlarge for a human, and thus far the suitcase had drawn no more attention than he had himself.

He poked at the bowl of rehydrated noodles in front of him and waved the waiter droid away when it approached. Through the window he saw the lights outside bay eighteen switch from green to red and the doors slam shut. A ship was coming in, and the bay would remain sealed until it had been cleared by the authorities. As he watched, a squad of stormtroopers took up a post outside the bay, eight of them in total, accompanied by two heavy-duty KX-series security droids. The stormtroopers split evenly into two groups of four at either side of the door, facing both directions along the promenade, on watch. One of them looked directly at him through the window, and Baze lowered his head back to his noodles and took a hearty slurp. When he glanced back again, the stormtrooper was once more focused on the activity on the promenade.

The door to the cantina slid open, and with it came

a blast of engine noise. Two men made their way to his booth and took the seat across from him.

"That's the ship," Leevan Tenza said.

Baze was looking at the other man, trying to place him. He was Trandoshan, and Baze was certain he had seen him before, but he couldn't place where or when. Just like Baze and Tenza, the Trandoshan wore a pilgrim's dust shroud drawn around him, over his clothes. Where it parted, Baze could see a cut-down CR-1 blast cannon strapped to his upper thigh. The Trandoshan met his eyes, held his gaze, then looked away. When he did, Baze could see the long scar running across his muzzle, splitting the scales, and he remembered Chirrut's hand on the man's face almost three months earlier, and he remembered his name and where he knew him.

"Wernad," Baze said. "You found a way to fight them."

The Trandoshan looked back at him. "Better than doing nothing."

"The others are in position," Tenza said. "Where are the kids?"

"Coming," Baze said.

"The timing has to be right. They can't be late."

"They know."

Outside, the doors to bay eighteen slid open, and

through them all three could see the *Sentinel*-class shuttle that had set down inside. There was a flurry of activity from the stormtroopers standing post, and half of the group, along with the KX droids, headed inside as two black-uniformed Imperial officers headed out. Tenza lowered his head as they passed the windows. Baze pulled a handful of credits from his pocket and stacked them on the table, then turned in his seat and leaned down to open his case. He snapped the latches back, took hold of the blaster cannon in his right hand and the coolant tank in his left, and stood up, back to the window.

Without another word, he walked to the doors of the cantina, stepped out into the promenade, and opened fire.

"How many kids?" Denic asked.

"Over thirty, now," Chirrut told her. "We will need a large vessel."

They were in Denic's garage, well past the middle of the night, the same night Baze had told Chirrut of his idea to evacuate the orphans. He and Chirrut had left the orphanage late, and only after Chirrut had checked to see that Althin had managed to fall asleep. The young

Rodian still hadn't said a word, but Kaya assured them that he had eaten, and that his arm would heal, and that, with time and opportunity, the deeper wounds of the day might heal, as well. That had been when Baze and Chirrut had asked her to join them, and Killi as well, and proposed the plan to get the children off the planet.

"Over thirty kids, how many adults?"

Chirrut hesitated. Baze waited. They had no answer to this as yet. Neither Killi nor Kaya wanted to leave the other behind, but it was clear that at least one of them would be required to go with the orphans, if not both. Even with the CZ droid's assistance, watching over that many children was a lot to ask of any adult. It was even more to ask of an adult who did not yet know where they might end up, nor who would care for the orphans when they arrived. And most of all, there was the very real question of whether whoever left with them would be coming back to Jedha at all.

"At least two," Chirrut said, finally.

"Either of these two adults a pilot?"

"No," Baze said.

"So you need a vessel to move—let's just say, I'm guessing here, but given the way things are working in this city lately, we'll round it up, okay?—forty people, mostly children. And you need a pilot to fly the thing. They bringing anything with them? Cargo?"

"Only essentials, what they will be able to carry with them."

Denic scratched her nose, adjusted her goggles. "Well, that's something, at least."

"What do you think?" Baze asked.

"I think you'll never get off the ground, that's what I think," she said. "The Imperials aren't going to give that many refugees clearance to depart, not with the way the situation here has deteriorated. Over thirty orphans? That gets onto the HoloNet, that's a public relations disaster for them, that gets attention in the Imperial Senate. You'll never get off the ground."

"We were thinking we would do this without clearance to depart," Chirrut said.

"You'll be shot from the skies before you leave the atmosphere. Anything big enough to move that many people, the TIEs will be all over it before you hit escape velocity. And that's if the Star Destroyer decides it's worth launching TIEs over. They could just as easily pick you off with any of their, how many . . ." She looked at her fingers, doing a quick count, then gave up. "There's a lot of turbolasers, that's how many. And quads. And heavy quads. And triples. All the guns, that's what I'm saying. That's if they want to shoot you. They might want to grab you instead, and then you're dealing with something like ten different tractor beams."

"We did not expect it would be easy to accomplish," Chirrut said. "But it is the only hope for these children."

"Yeah, Chirrut, you're not listening to me. I didn't say it wasn't going to be easy. I'm telling you it's next to impossible."

"Next to impossible."

"That's what I just said."

"There is a space between 'next to impossible' and 'impossible.'" Chirrut smiled at something only he knew was there. "That is where we will fit."

"This guy, you believe this guy?" Denic said to Baze.

"Yes," Baze said. "We will need a pilot."

Denic leaned back on the crate she'd perched upon, sucked on her lower lip for a moment, thinking. "You could try Barso. For enough credits he'd do it."

"Barso."

"Woan Barso. He's got that old Unar-Con tug he uses to move cargo up to the orbiting freighters. I've heard he'll take refugees up with him so they can stow away. That is, if the price is right."

"This is the Woan Barso who is always wearing that vac-suit?" Baze asked. "The filthy orange one? The one he never takes off?"

"That's him."

"Chirrut doesn't trust him," Baze said.

"Why not?"

"The vac-suit," Chirrut said. "Woan Barso either does not trust his skills or does not trust his ship, and putting the lives of these children in such hands would be, I think you will agree, foolish."

Denic sucked on her lower lip again for a moment. "Well, yeah, when you put it like that."

"We had someone else in mind," Baze said.

"I'm all ears."

Chirrut pointed his staff at Denic.

"You," he said.

The Morellian jumped in Baze's hand, spitting out bolt after bolt, the coolant tank in his other knocking against his thigh. That he could control the weapon at all one handed surprised Baze, but he hadn't wanted to risk being spotted while mounting the tank onto his back, and so he had decided to risk it. He had always been a strong man, stronger in his youth, but it pleased him somewhat that, even now, he could manage the weapon and make it do as he wished.

It did precisely as he wished. The bolts flew unerringly to target, and Baze worked left to right as he exited the cantina, sending stormtrooper after stormtrooper to the ground.

Tenza and Wernad were right behind him, and they each moved precisely as planned. From beneath his cloak, Tenza produced his rifle in two segments, quickly snapped the barrel into place on the receiver, and brought it to his shoulder, covering the promenade to the left. Wernad raised the cut-down blast cannon in both hands, covering the right. Baze headed straight to the entrance of bay eighteen, turning at the last moment to use the wall beside the door as cover, where he crouched on his haunches and threw his dust shroud over his shoulder.

"Clear left," Tenza said.

"Clear right," Wernad said.

"Hold," Baze said, swinging the tank onto his back and activating the magnetic clamps that would hold it in place. From within the docking bay all of them could hear the commotion and confusion of the stormtroopers who had entered with the droids, reacting to the noise from outside. The shooting had been intense, but brief, and they were only beginning to react. The crackle of comms ran in a ripple, helmet to helmet on each fallen stormtrooper as their fellow troopers inside tried to reach them. Baze checked the charging gauge on the Morellian, got back to his feet.

"Moving," he said, and pivoted into the doorway, the weapon now in both hands, thumb slapping the actuator below the electroscope on the cannon, initiating the smart targeting. If anything, he was more accurate this time than before, the cannon steady in his hands. Four shots, and four more stormtroopers were down, but it took Baze a half dozen more bolts before both of the KX-series droids stopped moving.

"Clear," Baze said, and stepped out of the way to let Tenza and Wernad run past, heading for the Sentinel. He waited until they were on the ramp, was sure they were both aboard, before turning back to the doorway to wait for Chirrut and the children.

"I cannot leave," Killi Gimm said. She raised her hands, palms turned up, as if to indicate that the decision was beyond her control.

Kaya looked to Baze for support, but Baze just

shook his head. This wasn't an argument he wanted a part of, and it was an argument that had been going on for a couple of weeks, now. It was an argument that had started immediately after he and Chirrut had proposed their plan to Killi and Kaya.

Kaya switched her appeal to Chirrut, then seemed to realize doing so was pointless and went back to her sister.

"You understand that staying here is killing you, right?" Kaya said.

"I understand that the air here is hurting me," Killi said. "Whether or not that will be what kills me remains to be seen."

"You can't ask me to go alone, Killi." Kaya's voice tightened with strain, and Baze could hear the tears in it. "You can't ask me to leave you like that."

Killi took her sister's hands.

"Would you two leave us alone for a little while, please?" she said.

Chirrut rose without a word and made his way to the door. Baze followed, closing it behind them. They stood in the largest room of the house, and several of the children were present. For a moment Baze and Chirrut were the center of all attention, but it quickly passed, and the children went back to what they had been doing prior. Baze and Chirrut's visits to the orphanage in the last several weeks had been so frequent that each of them had ceased to be a novelty.

"Althin," Baze said, and touched Chirrut's shoulder lightly, orienting him to where the boy was sitting, alone.

"He still does not speak to anyone," Chirrut said.

"You should talk to him."

Chirrut's expression tightened for a moment. He shook his head. "I have long since exhausted those things I can say to him. He knows I am here."

"He is a child," Baze said.

"He is a child who lost his parents. The words of an old Guardian offer him little."

"Are you angry at him, or . . . ?"

"I am not angry at him."

Baze sighed heavily, leaned his shoulder against the wall. Through the closed door, he could hear Kaya's voice rising, and the notes of emotion in it.

"They will not see each other again," Chirrut said.

"Why not?"

"Because Kaya is correct. Killi is dying. And Killi will not leave. This is her home, she is a Disciple of the

Whills. Kaya is younger, healthier. She is intelligent, resourceful, compassionate. She has skills she can sell, she understands machines, droids. Wherever Kaya and the children end up, she will be able to find their way. If Killi were to accompany her, Kaya's attention would be divided. As Killi's condition grows worse—and it will grow worse, we both know it, even if she does leave Jedha—Kaya's concern will grow. She will not be able to tend to her sister and the children at the same time. And the children must come first."

Baze just looked at him.

"Why are you staring at me?"

"That was remarkably cold."

Chirrut shook his head slightly, frowning. Baze tried to remember the last time he'd seen Chirrut happy.

"Kaya will need someone else to help," Baze said. "At least one other."

"She will have Denic. Denic will not be coming back, either."

"Why do you say that?"

"I know."

"How?"

Chirrut shrugged.

"You are beginning," Baze said, "to either worry me, or annoy me. I am not sure which."

"I suspect both."

The door opened, and Killi stepped out. Past her, Baze could see Kaya, sitting, her face in her hands, her elbows on her knees. Her body was shaking, but she made no sound as she wept.

"Kaya will go," Killi said. "I will stay."

Baze grunted.

"Now," Killi said. "How are we going to get all of these children aboard a stolen Imperial shuttle?"

We are awash in emotion, every day, every moment.

We are buffeted, we are confused, and sometimes,

yes, we are consumed.

When the pond is disturbed, we cannot see within.

When the pond is still, we can see with clarity.

In both instances, the water is still there.

So too is the Force like the water,

whether you see it clearly or not.

—Dejammy Shallon, teacher and priestess of D'janis IV
From *Collected Poems, Prayers, and Meditations on the Force*,
Edited by Kozem Pel, Disciple of the Whills

CHAPTER 12

IT WAS, WITHOUT QUESTION, one of the strangest things the people of the Holy City had witnessed since the start of the Imperial occupation.

It began in the midafternoon, and at first the only reactions were curiosity, perhaps amusement. The sight of thirty-four children, ages ranging from six standard years at the youngest to perhaps fourteen or fifteen at the oldest. Boys and girls, all manner of species—humans, Rodians, at least one Togruta, a Bith, a pair of Zabrak twins—all of them walking together. They formed not so much a column as a mass, making their way past the Division Wall and through the New Market and into the Old, and they walked without speaking. Only four adults were among them, and that was perhaps stranger still to the people who recognized them.

There was Killi Gimm, known to many as a Disciple of the Whills, recognizable even with the respirator mask hiding her features, wearing the red robes of her order. She was a tall woman, and being surrounded on all sides by children only made her appear taller. Walking with her, holding her hand, was Kaya Gimm, her younger sister—shorter, dressed in the same blue mechanic jumpsuit she always seemed to wear, tool belt around her waist, a satchel slung over her shoulder, held in place with her free hand. Some observers, catching a better look at Kaya, thought that her eyes were tearing, most likely due to the dust in the air. The wind was strong that afternoon, blowing steadily with occasional sharp gusts across the mesa. The Imperial flags that had been raised over the Old Market snapped loudly in the breeze.

Most of the people who saw the procession couldn't identify the other woman in the group, taking up the rear. This was because a great many of the people who could identify her had been arrested over the last several weeks and were now far, far from Jedha, likely never to return; and those who had managed to evade the stormtroopers thus far, had they been asked, would have categorically denied knowing her. She wore a set of goggles over her eyes, with a shock of strikingly red hair that seemed to erupt from her scalp at all angles. She wore traveling clothes, a thick spacer's jacket and pants and boots, and she had the holster for a blaster strapped to her thigh, but the holster itself was empty. She wore the clothes as if familiar in them, as if, perhaps, they had been all around the galaxy with her, and would be again.

But it was the man leading the procession who earned the most curiosity, the most scrutiny. He was known to many, if not by name then by sight. He had, until recently, taken to spending much of his days in the Old Market, with an alms bowl in one hand and a well-worn and carefully crafted uneti-wood staff in the other. Some said he was blind. Others said that was just an act, an attempt to prey upon people's good natures while he begged for money. Just watch him getting around, those same people said. If he's blind, I'm the Emperor.

A few claimed that he was a Guardian of the Whills, or had been before the Empire had sealed the Temple of the Kyber. Most dismissed this out of hand. The rumor was that the Guardians had all left Jedha when the Empire had arrived, and in fact there were many

in the Holy City who resented this. They felt that, like the Jedi Knights before them, the Guardians had abandoned the people in their hour of need.

Watching the man leading them, though, it was easy to believe that he could, indeed, see. He walked with purpose, without hesitation, the stick gently swaying bare centimeters above the ground in one hand, the hand of a young Rodian boy, perhaps no more than eight years old, in the other.

They walked, and sometimes Killi Gimm would have to pause, and she could be heard coughing behind her respirator, and when that happened the entire procession paused for her. Her sister would hold Killi's hand a little tighter. Then the fit would pass, and they would resume, and as they made their way through the Old Market and onto the Blessing Way, people began to follow them. A handful, at first, and then more and more, and more, none of them knowing where, precisely, they were going, nor what would happen when they got there. Following the man who might not have been blind at all.

It was not, after all, unheard of to see a progression of pilgrims making their way through the Holy City. Before the Empire had come, it had been common for both the Beatifics and the followers of the Isopter to walk the city. But that had not happened in years, and never could anyone remember the procession being made up almost entirely of children.

The stormtroopers noticed this, of course, and began relaying reports back to their command posts, comlinks crackling with messages ranging from bemusement to confusion. Should they be responding? What would they be responding to? How? Yes, one sergeant pointed out that technically, this *was* an illegal gathering. The Empire had decreed that no large groups were allowed to congregate in the Holy City until the current crisis with the partisans—whom they called terrorists—was resolved. But these were *children*, and none of them was armed as best as anyone could tell, and what were they going to arrest them for? If the procession had been making toward one of the command posts, or one of the designated LZs, that would have been different. Even walking to one of the old temples, certainly, their orders would have been clear, they'd have known how to respond.

But these children were just walking, following the maybe-not-so-blind man on some strange, circuitous route through the city.

By the time the procession reached the Square of

Stars, they had over fifty people trailing along behind them. When they left the Blessing Way the number had easily doubled, and by the time they turned onto Pilgrim's Walk, there were over two hundred of the Holy City's inhabitants following them.

By the time the stormtroopers realized they were heading to the spaceport, there were almost five hundred of them, and by then, it was far too late.

The biggest problem, it turned out, hadn't been how to get ahold of a ship, or whom they could find to fly the ship, or where they would take the ship, or who might join them on the journey.

The biggest problem, it turned out, was how to get the children on the ship in the first place.

It had been Beezer Fortuna who supplied the intelligence about the Sentinel shuttle. There was, he said, a regular run every third day of the week that brought command staff to Jedha. Their only cargo was the occasional piece of specialized mining equipment and replacement parts for the crystal matrix evaluators that were used to check the integrity of the kyber crystals. While the cargo was unloaded and distributed, the officers aboard would disembark to make inspection of the operation on Jedha. They would visit each of the LZs and command posts in turn, review the stormtroopers, and finally venture out of the Holy City—accompanied by heavily armed escort—to see firsthand the operation at each of the kyber mines. The visit, according to Fortuna, normally took between four and six hours, depending on what difficulties the inspecting officers might discover. More crucially, however, was the fact that the Sentinel didn't come down from the Star Destroyer overhead, but rather arrived from somewhere out of system. Beezer didn't know from where.

Frankly, it didn't matter.

What mattered—*all* that mattered—was that it was a Sienar Fleet Systems *Sentinel*-class shuttle, designed to carry up to seventy-five stormtroopers into battle, with Imperial command clearances for the skies over Jedha. It was expected. It was known. Every third day, it came out of hyperspace and into Jedha's airspace, and it flew right past the Star Destroyer, and everyone aboard that Star Destroyer overhead just smiled and nodded and said how nice it was to see you again, sir.

* * *

"They don't really say that," Chirrut said.

"It's an expression," Fortuna said.

Chirrut rubbed his chin. "It would be nice if they *did* say that."

"Ignore him," Baze said. "Go on."

Since the visit was an inspection, the officers didn't arrive with their own security contingent, Fortuna explained. They relied instead on the local garrison, and even that was token until they headed out of the city. As for the shuttle, once it was unloaded, there was barely a guard force left at the spaceport, only enough to keep the landing bay secure, and the pilot, who remained aboard the ship per Imperial protocol just in case the officers needed to depart in a hurry.

The shuttle was just sitting there.

If it could be secured quickly, relatively quietly, and if it lifted off again roughly close to when it was expected to depart, nobody would raise an eyebrow.

But that was the complication. Lifting off from the spaceport and leaving the moon wouldn't raise suspicion. But if Denic instead lifted off only to buzz half the Holy City and then set down outside the orphanage to take on passengers, it didn't matter how quickly they could get the children aboard.

Somebody was going to notice, and noticing would lead to questions, and questioning would lead to TIE fighters.

A *Sentinel*-class shuttle versus a Star Destroyer's complement of TIE fighters would only end one way.

"Boom," said Chirrut.

"Boom," agreed Denic.

Several plans were suggested as to how to move the children to the shuttle, or the shuttle to the children.

They spent a week trying to determine if it would be possible to commandeer one of the assault tanks, perhaps, and use that to clear a run to the spaceport. Baze went so far as to begin plotting possible routes to use before that line of thinking was abandoned. Kaya suggested they try to acquire landspeeders, four or five of them, but the streets were so regularly congested that it would require boosting the repulsorlift fields on the vehicles until they could essentially fly. That would bring the TIEs for a visit, and quickly.

It was actually Denic who suggested using the partisans to start some manner of distraction in another part of the city, perhaps down by the South Wall. While the Imperials were occupied, Denic could bring the shuttle in low, and if they loaded everyone aboard quickly . . .

"There are over thirty children," Killi said.

"I know," Denic said.

"Have you ever tried to get thirty children to do anything quickly?" Killi asked.

"Point taken," Denic said.

It was Gerrera, via Fortuna, who suggested they just walk.

"The General believes that even Imperial stormtroopers will hesitate to open fire on children who are simply out for a walk." Fortuna always referred to Gerrera as "the General." "Even if they wished to, doing so in broad daylight in front of the local populace would be a deliberately inciting act of violence. They'd have a riot on their hands."

"You seem to think that would bother them," Baze said.

"It would if *they* were the cause of it in such an

obvious manner," Fortuna said. "A child dies in the street, caught in the crossfire? That's a tragedy, but they overlook it. They blame us, not themselves. They blame us for fighting their tyranny. If we had just accepted their boot on our neck, this would never have happened, they say. But in numbers? Unarmed? Doing nothing but walking to a spaceport? That would be a *war crime*."

"If you're wrong?" Chirrut asked.

Fortuna just shook his head. He didn't want to say it.

Chirrut considered the idea for a very long time. He and Baze discussed it at length. Then he brought it to Killi and Kaya, and all four of them discussed it all over again, and none of them liked it, either. But they all also agreed that it was the least risky of their options, as well as the one most likely to succeed.

"But if it goes wrong . . ." Kaya said.

"This," Chirrut said, "is what is called a test of faith."

Chirrut led the way beneath the ancient stone archway into the spaceport, Althin's hand in his, the other children following close behind. He felt Althin's grip on him tighten, understood at once that the boy had seen the stormtroopers posted at the entrance, and he thought he could feel the stormtroopers, as well, watching them. But the stormtroopers didn't move, and didn't challenge them. By this point, Chirrut reasoned, they surely had heard any comm traffic flying around the city about the strange parade he was leading.

He had no idea how many people were following behind them now, but he knew there were a great many. He could feel them, the essence and energy of them, pressing at his back like a wind filling a sail.

"It will be fine," Chirrut told Althin. "Trust in the Force."

The ground changed beneath his feet, the old stonework streets of the city giving way to the brickwork of the spaceport's promenade. Ahead of him, not so far away now, was Baze. Ahead of him, not so far away now, was their goal.

He hoped he would have the courage to do what was required when they reached it.

There was noise rising behind him, a mixture of voices, far too many to make out. They held some urgency, yet seemed shy of anger.

"What is happening?" he asked Althin. "What is happening behind us?"

Another child, to his right, answered, and he

recognized her voice at once. It was B'asia, the Togruta who had been hurt when the stormtroopers raided the first orphanage.

"The people following us, there're too many of them, Master Îmwe," she said. "They can't all get through the archway, they're all . . . they're getting stuck." She giggled. "The stormtroopers don't know what to do!"

"There must be a great many of them," Chirrut said.

"I think half the city is following us, Master Îmwe!"

"We are looking for number eighteen, B'asia. Do you see it?"

"Yes, it's up ahead. It's right over here. I can see Master Malbus!"

He heard the girl surging forward, the sound of her steps, and he felt Althin tugging at his hand, the boy similarly speeding up. As their pace increased, so too did that of those following them, and the echo-box and Althin told him at the same time to turn, and he felt the space around them opening, the sound altering as the roof above them gave way to the sky. The hangar bay had its own distinct feel, almost cavernous, and it played with sound, and for an instant he was unsure whether it was his own senses or the echo-box or both that confused him, threatened to disorient him for an instant. Althin stopped short. Chirrut could feel the energy around him, the living energy, the Force moving between beings, and he found Baze at once, knew him instantly, as he always did when his connection was strong.

But there was a chill, and it wasn't from the air, and it wasn't from his friend.

Something was wrong.

"Baze Malbus," Chirrut said.

"Gerrera's men," Baze said. "They're taking the shuttle."

The Force is with me,

and I am one with the Force;

and I fear nothing,

because all is as the Force wills it.

—The Guardian's Mantra, author unknown
From *Collected Poems, Prayers, and Meditations on the Force,*
Edited by Kozem Pel, Disciple of the Whills

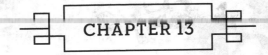

TENZA AND WERNAD had boarded the Sentinel as planned, and Baze had moved to cover the entrance. Then he heard the blaster shot, muffled from within the shuttle, and he turned back to see them dragging the body of the pilot to the ramp and dumping him onto the floor of the hangar bay.

Baze practically snarled. "There was no need for that!"

Tenza sneered at him. "He was Imperial. If it bothers you, be assured I made it quick. I could have made him suffer."

"Watch the entrance," Baze told Wernad. He holstered the Morellian and moved to the pilot's body. Their plan had been to restrain the pilot, keep him in binders aboard the shuttle in case they needed him to help fly the ship, or to provide any Imperial clearances they might need. Then Denic and Kaya would release him whenever they reached their destination. Now, Baze's immediate thought was of the children and what they would see when they arrived. He didn't want them having to step over a fresh corpse to board the Sentinel.

The floor of the hangar bay was stone, worn smooth by age and countless landings and takeoffs, and here and there it shone as reflective as glass. The pilot's helmet was still in place, but his body was already cooling as Baze hoisted him over his shoulder. He moved the body off to the side of the bay, out of the direct line of sight, set him down, and then went back and did the same for each of the stormtroopers. He was aware of Wernad glancing from the entrance of the bay and back to him as he worked. Tenza had disappeared back into the shuttle. He could hear noise from the promenade, a growing wave of sound, and he knew that Chirrut and the children and Killi and Kaya and Denic, all of them, had to be close, would be here in minutes.

Baze had just finished shifting the last of the bodies when more of Gerrera's men arrived, this time Fortuna and Sperado. Each had a large satchel slung across his back. They passed Wernad without stopping, heading straight for the shuttle's ramp. Baze moved to intercept them.

"You're supposed to be watching their approach," Baze said. "In case they need support."

"They do not need support," Fortuna said, and tried to get around him, but Baze adjusted and didn't let him pass. "They will be here in moments. Everything is going according to plan."

"Whose plan?"

"The General's plan, of course."

"The General's plan was to get these children off Jedha."

"No," Fortuna said. "That was *your* plan. This is too great an opportunity to ignore. We must seize it."

Baze started forward, reaching for the Morellian on his back, but there was no way it would be a quick draw, and his hand wasn't halfway to the cannon before Sperado had his blaster free from its holster and pointed at his middle. Baze froze. Fortuna shook his head slightly.

"I was afraid this might happen." The Twi'lek looked at Sperado. "Keep him here. Give me your satchel."

Sperado slipped the strap off his shoulder and handed the satchel to Fortuna, his aim never wavering. Fortuna headed for the shuttle. The sound off the promenade had expanded, growing even louder. Chirrut and the children were close now, very close, and who knew how many others were coming with them.

"There are thirty-four children coming," Baze said. "They are on their way. And they will see you holding your gun on me. Is that what you want them to see?"

Sperado hesitated, then stepped back and reholstered his blaster as smoothly as he had drawn it.

"I really don't want to have to shoot you," Sperado said.

Baze didn't bother with an answer, just started for the entrance into the bay. He was halfway there when the Togruta girl came into sight, rounding the corner, and then Althin, pulling on Chirrut's hand. More of the children were right behind them, and they all were funneling into the bay, and Chirrut was heading toward him. He could see it in Chirrut's face, the brief furrowing of his brow, the tightening of his lips into a line. He knew something was wrong; he didn't need Baze to say it.

But Baze said it anyway.

"Gerrera's men," Baze said. "They're taking the shuttle."

* * *

Chirrut's expression went flat for an instant. Beside him, still holding his hand, Althin's eyes widened, seemed to double in size. Chirrut slipped his hand free from the boy's, both of his own coming together on his staff. Past him, Baze could now see Killi and Kaya, and Denic at the back, ushering the children forward. Confused expressions on their faces turned to worry.

"No," Chirrut said. "They shall not."

He started forward, and Baze turned to walk beside him. After a moment's hesitation Althin followed, and as soon as he moved, so did the others. Sperado came around to their left side, trying to keep pace. He wore, Baze saw, twin blasters, a double rig worn quick-draw style, and his furred hands hovered over their grips, but he had yet to draw. Wernad was hurrying to catch up, to flank them on their right.

"Master Îmwe," Sperado said. "Please, do not do this."

"These children have walked the length of the city," Chirrut said, without breaking his stride. "They have been promised a ride in a shuttle for their efforts. I do not wish to see them disappointed. Do you, Kullbee Sperado?"

"Don't let them on board. You cannot let them on board."

They were approaching the base of the loading ramp, now. Baze looked back, saw that all the children, Killi, Kaya, Denic—everyone was with them. Past them, the entrance to the bay was absolutely clogged with men and women, citizens of Jedha trying to see what was going on.

"Stormtroopers will be here soon," Baze said.

"It will take them a while to disperse the crowd," Chirrut said.

"Provided they don't do it violently."

Chirrut nodded slightly. To Sperado, he said, "Why?"

Fortuna, at the top of the ramp, answered for him.

"Because the people need a symbol of hope," the Twi'lek said. He spoke loudly, projecting for everyone in the bay to hear him. The low rumble of voices died away, people falling silent to listen. "Saw Gerrera will give them one."

"These children *are* a symbol of hope," Baze said.

"Look!" Fortuna pointed skyward, and everyone listening looked up.

All of them except for Chirrut, and perhaps because of that, Chirrut understood precisely what it was Gerrera wanted to do.

"Look at the symbol of your oppression!" Fortuna

shouted. "How it hangs over all your heads, how it casts its shadow over all of your lives! We cannot live this way! We must fight them!"

There was a ripple of confusion through the crowd. Althin reached for Chirrut's hand and instead took hold of his robe at the elbow, gripping it tight.

"Just how large does an explosive need to be to bring down a Star Destroyer?" Chirrut asked.

The murmuring, the voices, all went suddenly, utterly silent.

"You'd need a pretty big one," Baze said. "If you loaded it onto a shuttle, you'd need to fly it right into the main hangar."

"Do you think that would do it?"

"It might."

"It will," Fortuna said.

"I see," Chirrut said.

He grinned as he said it. Baze—despite everything going on around them, despite the hundreds of people behind them, and the children, and Killi, and Kaya, and Denic, despite the fact that they were rapidly running out of time before the stormtroopers broke through the human shield that the citizens of the Holy City had made for them—felt himself grinning as well.

"So Saw Gerrera would trade a future for these children to strike a blow against the Empire?" Chirrut asked.

Fortuna jabbed a long-nailed index finger skyward again. "He would free Jedha!"

"That is not what will happen," said Baze.

"My friend is correct," Chirrut said. "And neither you, nor Saw Gerrera, nor anyone else here is fool enough to think that it will."

"We must fight them!" Fortuna said.

The words made Chirrut straighten slightly. He canted his head.

"Wernad," Chirrut said. "Is that you? I think I feel you here."

"Yes," the Trandoshan said. His voice was almost a whisper, and yet it carried throughout the hangar. "I am here."

"You said the same thing to me."

"I did, I remember."

"And now you do, it seems. And this is how you will do it. Do you remember what I said to you?"

"'Not with the innocent,'" Wernad said.

Chirrut nodded to himself, canted his head the other direction. "You asked me to pray for you, Kullbee Sperado. Is this the place you were looking for?"

Sperado did not answer.

Chirrut extended his hand to the side, holding his walking stick. Baze took it from him. Chirrut dropped to his haunches, wrapped his arms around Althin, and lifted the boy, holding him much as he had the day he had found him, weeping, over his parents. The arm had healed well. The other wounds had not, yet.

"They were promised a ride in a shuttle," Chirrut said to Baze.

"And you cannot stand to disappoint them."

Chirrut's grin was almost gleeful. "You know me very well."

"Right," Baze said. He turned and faced the children. "Come on, then."

Chirrut started up the ramp, and Baze took the Togruta girl's hand and followed. Fortuna stepped out of Chirrut's way, realized what he was doing, and started to move back to block Baze.

"Think about everyone who is watching us." Baze met Fortuna's eyes. His voice was level. His voice was calm. Yet each word seemed to have his entire weight, all his strength, standing behind it. "And then think, very carefully, about what the General would want you to do next."

"The General will never forgive this."

"He won't have to," Baze said. "Our relationship with Saw Gerrera is over."

Fortuna hesitated.

Then he moved out of the way.

Baze led the girl into the shuttle and was only mildly surprised to see that Sperado and Wernad had followed them. More and more children were ushered aboard, Killi and Kaya moving among them, getting them into their seats. Chirrut was crouched on his haunches, facing Althin, now seated as well. Denic ascended the ramp but had to step out of the way as Tenza was ushered out by Wernad and Sperado, each of them carrying one of the satchels.

"Tell me those were the bombs," Denic said.

"Those," Baze said, "were the bombs."

"One less thing to worry about." She started for the cockpit, stopped. "We have three minutes, tops, before the stormtroopers decide that they've had enough of playing nice. Which means we've got two minutes to get out of here. Everyone get buckled up and say your good-byes."

Killi was at the top of the ramp with Kaya. She had

removed her respirator mask and was kissing her sister on the forehead. They embraced. Baze looked back to Chirrut, saw that he was giving Althin a hug. The boy was whispering something to him, and whatever he was saying made his friend smile.

"And I fear nothing," Chirrut said. "Because all is as the Force wills it."

Chirrut rose, moved to where Baze was standing, and Baze held out his walking stick, and Chirrut took it without hesitation. Beneath their feet, they felt a slight vibration as the primary repulsorlift systems came online, the engines beginning to power up.

"I'm going to miss you," Chirrut said to Baze.

Baze smiled, then realized what Chirrut was actually saying, and said, "No, no. *I* am going to miss *you*."

"Don't be absurd. You must go with them."

"No, *you* must go with them. It is for the best. They need your guidance."

"This is not the time to argue with me, Baze Malbus. Here, your anger only grows. You must leave Jedha before it consumes you."

"You cannot be left alone," Baze said. "You would walk into walls."

"I have not walked into a wall unintentionally in twenty years."

"Yes, because I am here to keep you from doing that."

"You must leave with them."

Killi's voice came up from the bottom of the ramp. "Don't be absurd, neither of you is going anywhere without the other. Which means you're both staying here."

"With Saw Gerrera angry at us on one side for spoiling his plans, and the Empire wanting our hides now on the other?" Baze shook his head.

"The Empire will never know who was truly responsible for this." Chirrut smirked. "They will blame Gerrera's partisans, and in part they will be correct, and Gerrera will not dispute it for all the obvious reasons. And because, in the end, even if we did not allow him what he wanted, he still can claim yet another blow struck against the Empire."

Baze grunted. "I really thought this was how I'd finally get rid of you."

Chirrut laughed and headed down the ramp, Baze beside him. There was still a substantial crowd clustered at the mouth of the hangar bay, but Baze could see neither Tenza nor Fortuna. He and Chirrut stood with Killi, and Wernad, and Sperado. Together they watched as the ramp lifted into place and, almost immediately, the shuttle shuddered and lifted into the air. It rose slowly, ascending straight up, rotating in place as it did so. It cleared the top of the bay, and its nose lifted, and the engines roared.

Along with almost everyone else in the hangar, Baze found he was holding his breath.

Chirrut and Killi were praying softly, repeating their mantras.

The shuttle's wings locked into flight position, and it banked gently, easily, as if it had all the time in the world. The shadow of the Star Destroyer fell over it, seemed to consume it, hiding it from view as the Sentinel passed underneath. Those who had lost sight of the shuttle instead turned their eyes to the hangar bay of the Star Destroyer.

But there were no TIEs to be seen.

No alarms could be heard.

Then the Sentinel was out of the shadow and into the sunlight, and the shuttle seemed to gleam in the sky as it accelerated, climbing faster and faster. Its shape grew less distinct, smaller and smaller, until it was a tiny speck, and then, an instant later, it was gone.

There was a moment of stillness, of silence in the hangar.

Baze and Chirrut could hear the stormtroopers approaching, the amplified voices shouting for people to clear the way. Hands reached for them out of the crowd, drew them in, wrapped them in anonymity. They saw Killi Gimm ushered away in one direction, found themselves shepherded along the promenade in another, until they were unknown and unnoticed once more.

Chirrut took a deep breath, let it go through his nose, settled his stance, his hands on his walking stick. Baze idly checked the Morellian in his hands and assured himself that it was fully charged.

"Tea?" Chirrut asked.

"Tarine?"

"Yes."

Baze grunted. "Fine."

They began the long walk home, through their city, together.

ABOUT THE AUTHOR

Credit: Jai Soots

Greg Rucka is a *New York Times* best-selling author of hundreds of comics and over two dozen novels, including the *Star Wars* books *Before the Awakening* and *Smuggler's Run*. He has written for film, television, and video games. He lives in Portland, Oregon, with his wife, author Jennifer Van Meter, and their two children, Elliot and Dashiell.